the CEMETERY BOYS

the CEMETERY BOYS

HEATHER BREWER

HARPER TEEN

An Imprint of HarperCollinsPublishers

HarperTeen is an imprint of HarperCollins Publishers.

The Cemetery Boys
Copyright © 2015 by Heather Brewer LLC
HarperCollins Children's Books, a division of HarperCollins Publishers,
195 Broadway, New York, NY 10007.
www.epicreads.com

Library of Congress Cataloging-in-Publication Data
Brewer, Heather.
    The cemetery boys / Heather Brewer.
        pages   cm
    ISBN 978-0-06-230788-0 (hardback)
    [1. Supernatural—Fiction.   2. Peer pressure—Fiction.   3. Dating
(Social customs)—Fiction.   4. Cults—Fiction.   5. Brothers and sisters—
Fiction.   6. Twins—Fiction.   7. Moving, Household—Fiction.   8. Horror
stories.]   I. Title.
PZ7.B75695Cem   2015   2014027404
[Fic]—dc23   CIP
                                                                 AC

Typography by Carla Weise
15 16 17 18 19   PC/RRDH   10 9 8 7 6 5 4 3 2 1

First Edition

To my grandma Elsie Westrick,
who passed down the writing gene
that I cherish so dearly.

And to my grandma Jessie Truax,
who taught me everything that I know
about family.

the CEMETERY BOYS

prologue

My fingers were going numb, my bound wrists worn raw by the ropes, but I twisted again, hard this time. I pulled until my skin must have split, because I felt my palms grow wet, then sticky, with what I was pretty sure was my blood. The knots were tight, but I had to get loose. Those *things* were coming for me, I just knew it.

I looked up at Devon, who was perched on top of the tallest tombstone in the graveyard. His dark eyes focused intensely on the night sky; his bleach-blond hair almost glowed in the moonlight. He had once—no, not once, many times, pounding it into our heads like we were privates in the same army—spoken of loyalty. But sitting there with my wrists tied to the cold headstone behind me, it hit me that he hadn't been speaking of our loyalty to one another or any of that band-of-brothers bullshit. He'd been speaking of our loyalty, my loyalty, to him. And now he was standing there on the gravestone, waiting for those creatures, those monsters, to come and devour me whole, not even man enough to look me in the eye.

The horrible pinpricks of numbness crawled up my fingers to my palms, then my wrists. Only my adrenaline kept them from going any farther. The air suddenly chilled. My breath came out in quick, gray puffs. And then I heard it.

Vwumph-vwumph-vwumph.

I tugged my wrists harder, struggling, hoping that the blood seeping from my broken skin might make the ropes slick enough to slip through. The rest of the gang moved past me, and none of them, not a single one of my so-called friends, dared even to glance at me as they headed for safety. Devon hopped down from his place on the stone, and after a long, hungry glance upward, he dropped his dark eyes to me. "You're in luck, Stephen. They're famished, so this should go pretty fast for you."

I bit down on my tongue, consumed with rage. A million curses ran through my mind, but I could barely speak through my fury—fury with him for all that he'd done, but mostly fury with myself for having followed his lead. I spat at him. "Go to hell!"

I pulled until I thought my shoulders might come out of their sockets, not caring that I was bleeding freely now, praying to anyone and anything that the knots would give way at last. But it was no use. The ropes refused to budge.

And then, the flapping stopped.

I looked up—up into the dark, my eyes settling on a shape in the night. And what I saw . . . oh god. My screams tore through me, my throat burning.

From the distance came Devon's laughter—cold, quiet, hollow—and his reply, muted by the sounds of my screams. "You first."

chapter 1

We'd left my old house as if we were stealing away in the night. Which, really, I guess we were. We'd driven out of Denver in the dark, stopping in Omaha, Chicago, and several forgettable truck stops over the course of the next day, coming full circle when we reached the sign at the edge of my new town at eleven thirty. Darkness to darkness. *Welcome to Spencer*, the sign had read. *Population 814.*

Shit.

It wasn't like I had anything against small towns in theory. But there were small towns . . . and then there was Spencer. My dad had grown up here, and every story he'd ever told me about his hometown had begun with an exhausted sigh and ended with the relief of moving away. So how else was I supposed to feel when Dad came to me a week ago and announced that moving to Spencer was the only answer, only option to contain the avalanche of debt that had befallen our family? I could still see him when I closed my eyes, standing there in the hall just outside my bedroom, his hair disheveled, a shaking hand clutching yet another stack of hospital bills. There was no arguing with him, but he acted like I was going to argue. "Stephen, we're moving in with my mother. We're moving to Spencer."

That was it. Just "we're moving." Just that.

After he said it, he'd looked at me, an almost angry glint in his eyes. I didn't say a word. There was no point. It was over. Our life in Denver, our hope that maybe Mom would get better, or Dad would find another job—it was all over. We were moving.

Finally, Dad had nodded, turning from my door. I'd listened to the sounds of his heavy footsteps retreating to his office down the hall. I'd had the same thought then that I had tonight upon seeing the *Welcome to Spencer* sign.

Shit.

As we pulled into the driveway, my dad started rambling about how my grandmother was very *particular* about the way she kept her home. That we couldn't leave a mess anywhere. There was no worry over meeting her just yet, as Dad explained she'd be out of town until Monday. It was the first piece of good news I'd heard the whole trip.

The rest of the night was a blur after that. Loading boxes into my grandmother's house, falling into bed in a strange room.

The blur was still with me the next morning when I cracked my eyes open—my first waking moment as a resident of Spencer, Michigan: population now 816. Guess they'd have to change the sign.

I held my hand up to the sunlight that was pouring in through my curtainless window and flipped it the bird. Morning came too early sometimes. I preferred night, when you've spent all day getting stuff done so that you can just bask in the darkness. Night hid the ugly of the world. And sometimes, when I was feeling ugly, I was grateful that it would hide me, too.

I gripped my pillow and yanked it out from under my head, placing it over my face. I'd better find the box of curtains before I went to bed again or the sun and I were going to have some serious issues.

I pressed the pillow down hard on my face until I felt a familiar sensation of panic wash over me. What a stupid thing to feel. Like I was really capable of suffocating myself. It was funny the things a person reacted to instinctively, without rational thought. Like when I'd take a shower and get water up my nose, for instance. It always felt like I was drowning. Maybe I hoped that I would. Maybe Dad was right and I had some kind of death wish. Maybe he'd moved us here in the dark of night hoping to give me some distance from the thoughts I wouldn't admit to having back home. But that's where he was wrong. I didn't need distance. I just wanted to feel normal again. The way I had before Mom started rambling about monsters. Before we'd had to have her medicated and locked away, so she wouldn't hurt herself . . . or us.

"Stephen, are you up yet? I could use some help out here." I tossed the pillow to the foot of the bed and glared at the sun. Morning, man. I needed a little less morning in my life.

I rolled out of bed, still yawning as I navigated the piles of boxes that were sitting in my way. Recognizing one of them by the word *Fragile* written on the side, I popped open the lid and took out a framed photo of my mom. In the picture, she was standing outside our house in Denver in a pile of fresh snow. I remembered Dad pegging her with a snowball right after I'd snapped it, and then we'd all gone inside and had hot cocoa. A smile threatened to lift my lips, but reality settled my mouth again. I set the picture on my nightstand and kept moving.

My dad was standing on a chair in the kitchen, carefully lifting Mom's favorite china teapot over his head. He was wearing jeans from back in his college days and a blue T-shirt, his feet clad in white sneakers with tiny polo guys stitched on the sides, which told me he was dressed for hard labor. It didn't bode well for my day. If he was unpacking, that meant that I was unpacking, too.

There was a space between the top of the cupboard and the ceiling, and apparently, he'd determined that it was a good place to put Mom's teapot on display. Maybe he thought it would be nice to have a reminder of her at the center of the house, an unspoken promise not to forget why we were here, all the while getting on with our lives.

I leaned against the kitchen table, which looked a bit like something I once saw on *The Twilight Zone*—on that episode where Captain Kirk gets advice from a devil fortune-telling machine. Dad and I used to watch that show together all the time. At first, I didn't really get it. A series of weird stories in black and white, featuring a guy named Rod Serling and always something bizarre, like aliens or robots or evil beings. But after a while, I realized how cool it was. Not just that I could see an evil kid wishing people he didn't like into a cornfield. That I had something I shared with my dad.

But that was before. Before our lives turned into an episode of *The Twilight Zone* and the show sort of lost its appeal.

Anyway, the table was totally retro. Chrome lined and shiny red, just like the four matching chairs. I plopped down on one of those chairs and yawned again, contemplating just how desperate someone would have to be to move to a town like Spencer. Pretty desperate, by the look of things.

From where I sat, I could see a pile of boxes near the front door. Most of our furniture was still on the truck. Dad had mentioned something about taking it to a storage unit today, so if I wanted anything for the foreseeable future, I'd better grab it this morning.

He turned the teapot slightly before climbing back down and admiring it. It was only then that he noticed me sitting at the table. "Oh, you're up. Good. Would you mind unpacking the sheets and towels, while I get all of my clothes put away? I don't want to be an inconvenience to your grandmother any more than we have to."

Grandmother. Right. He was referring to the woman who hadn't reached out to me, her only grandson, even once in my entire life. I'd hate to inconvenience *her*.

A sigh escaped me. "Can I get breakfast first?"

"Help me with this stuff and I'll take you out to eat. Besides, there's not really anything of ours to eat here at the house just yet. We still have to go grocery shopping, and everything has to be put away and taken care of before your grandmother gets back tomorrow." He was wearing his expectant look again. The same look that he'd been wearing two days ago when he told me we'd better hurry up and get the moving truck packed or we'd never make it to Spencer.

Promises, promises.

My stomach rumbled vaguely, and I thought about the half-empty bag of beef jerky I'd shoved into the glove box of the moving truck last night. "I'm starving."

"You'll live. At least long enough to get off your butt and put the towels away. They go in the closet across the hall from your room. Our sheets and blankets go in the closet across from my room. Get moving." He nodded to the boxes by the front door. It took an effort for me not to point out just how stupid this whole endeavor was. We were only supposed to be here as long as it took for Dad to find another job. Nobody would invite someone to stay in their home and expect them to bring their own towels. Would they? And what was that crack about buying our own groceries before we ate anything? What, was my grandmother going to freak out and start throwing things if I grabbed a bowl of cereal that I hadn't actually purchased? What kind of nuthouse had he moved us to?

With a grunt, I stood up and moved to the pile by the front door. If I was a couple of towels and some sheets away from getting a Sausage McMuffin, you could bet I was going to knock that job out so I could get on with my day.

After locating the knife my dad had given me when I was twelve—*"Every boy needs a knife, Stephen"*—I sliced open the linens box and pulled out the pile of sheets and pillowcases inside. I lugged them down the hall and crammed them into the closet. Shoving the door closed, I said a small prayer for whoever opened that door after me. Not that I was the religious type.

Then, I found the box containing our towels and shuffled them to the closet Dad had mentioned. I actually managed to finish before I starved to death, which was pretty amazing, if you asked me.

I walked into the kitchen and looked at my dad expectantly, without saying a word. He nodded. "Okay. Go take your shower and we'll eat. There's a diner on the other end of town."

There was only one bathroom in the house, which I could already see was going to be a problem. My grandmother had claimed every inch of the medicine cabinet as her own, and the small cabinet by the pedestal sink was already full of things like bubble bath and body lotion. The tub was a huge claw-footed monstrosity, and when I turned the water on, the curtain that hung around it from an oval ring up above sucked inward, like it was trying to suffocate anyone who climbed inside. There was no way I could have hated this bathroom more.

That is, until I noticed my grandmother had stuck pink

plastic daisies all over the bottom of the tub and hung an annoying plaque on the wall behind the toilet that read *If you sprinkle when you tinkle, be a sweetie and wipe the seatie.*

The words *die already* came to mind, but I wasn't certain who my brain was directing them at.

I hurried through a shower, fighting the curtain's murderous advances the entire time, and threw on some clean clothes—just jeans and a T-shirt, nothing fancy. If the good citizens of Spencer wanted me to dress up for Sunday breakfast, I had a few ideas for where the good citizens of Spencer could stick it.

I wasn't really sure what to expect from Spencer, though. After Dad had told me that we were moving to the capital of midwestern nowhere, I'd Googled the town, hoping to find something salvageable for my summer. But the only things that had turned up had been a Wikipedia page stating that the "village" was about a square mile in *total*, and the town's website, which featured a quaint photograph of the town's reservoir and an announcement of when the next First Baptist euchre tournament would be.

So I would have been lying if I said that I wasn't at least a little curious about the place my father had chosen as our new home. I threw on a pair of Chucks and grabbed my wallet from my bedroom before heading out to the kitchen, ready for anything.

Anything would have been nice. Hell, even *something* would have been acceptable. But as we navigated the streets in my dad's beat-up '73 Volkswagen Beetle—stylin' in baby blue and rust so bad that the car looked more Swiss than German—I had a first-row seat to the nothing show of the century. Spencer's streets looked as if they hadn't been redone in several decades. Where there weren't potholes, there were layers of patch so thick that they made small hills in the road. Spencer's sidewalks had been shifted and lifted by the roots of the unkempt trees that grew along two main thoroughfares. At the center of town, encaged by a rusted, wrought-iron fence, stood an old brick mansion that had seen better days. The building reminded me of a woman who had been a real beauty in her younger years, but now denied the fact that those days were long gone. I wondered if she was a reflection of the rest of her town. I hoped not. I hoped that Spencer had something more to offer.

As we passed a run-down gas station, I rolled my eyes at the faded Confederate flag hanging in the window. Who displayed something like that so prominently and thought it was okay?

The three old men standing outside eyed our vehicle distrustfully. I sank down in my seat, pretending not to notice. We were the new people here. We weren't part of their group. We had to prove ourselves worthy of their small-town ways. I didn't even want to think about what the school year would be like if we were still here this fall. If the adults stared us down this bad, what would the high schoolers be like?

The other side of the gas station was home to graffiti—nothing special, just a large, roughly painted pair of stark black wings. Probably Spencer's idea of what passed for small-town rebellion, when in fact the teenage punks were all just farmers' kids or a close variation thereof. These kids had no idea what punk was, what a big city was. Kids in Denver would eat them alive.

As Dad pulled into the surprisingly full parking lot of the Lakehouse Grill, he grimaced. "I swear this town never changes. It looks the same as it did the day I left."

I caught sight of two bumper stickers on the truck next to us. One read *Pro Life: Have a heart. Don't stop one.* The other read *Keep honking. I'm reloading.*

Awesome. Just . . . awesome.

I opened the passenger door of the Beetle, hoping like hell the rust would hold it together and the door wouldn't fall off completely. I climbed out, closing the door behind me with a slam. It was the only way to be sure the stupid thing would close at all. My actions apparently caught the attention of a group of four kids around my age as they exited the restaurant, because all four were staring at me and my dad's crappy car. One of the three guys in the group—tall, tan, and probably into things like Ultimate Frisbee and racquetball—whistled at the rust monstrosity as he slipped his arm around the slender, just as tan, likely-into-gymnastics-and-discussing-everything-to-do-with-her-hair girl in the group. An embarrassed heat worked its way up my neck as we walked by them and headed inside. I hated the Beetle. I hated the way those kids had noticed it, had noticed me. My dad seemed oblivious to the stares.

The Lakehouse Grill was small-town chic . . . in that it had panel-covered walls from the seventies, ripped-vinyl booth seats, and enough fake plants to choke a horse. A weird horse that ate fake plants. Probably a horse from small-town Michigan.

As far as I had seen, it seemed like it was pretty much our only option for eating out unless we wanted to drive thirty minutes to the next town over, so I was hoping they had some fair-to-decent food. When we stepped inside, we were greeted by a woman who was basically every hostess in every small-town café everywhere. She was relatively short and relatively thin, and I could tell by her gravelly voice that she smoked way too many cigarettes when she wasn't busy directing people where to sit. Around her neck she wore a pair of reading glasses on a chain. A younger, much prettier blond lady was arguing quietly with her. The hostess was losing her cool. "I know, Marjorie, but Spencer's going through a bad time right now. You just have to be more careful is all. It'll all be over soon. Now get your buns back in the kitchen."

She looked at my dad expectantly. "Two?"

"Yes, please." We followed her into the main dining area, to a booth near the back. As we moved, I could feel eyes on me, wondering just who we were and what we thought we were doing here. Maybe some of these people recognized Dad or something. But from the look on Dad's face as we moved past the tables, it was clear that he didn't recognize any of them.

The hostess handed us menus and told us that Donna would be taking care of us, then she called me "honey," and, even resistant to her chain-smoking charms as I was, it felt nice. Maybe she could speak to the gas station guys on our behalf and tell them that my dad and I weren't so bad. Or at least get the patrons to stop staring.

Dad peered over his menu at me and cleared his throat. "It would be nice if you called your mom when we get back, and let her know we made it okay."

It was a nudge. I'd become very familiar with his nudges in the past six months. He'd nudge me to call her, to make a connection, to try to forgive her for the things she couldn't control. But I wasn't ready yet. So as usual, I countered his nudge with a lie. "Yeah. Maybe. I don't know. We've got all that unpacking to do."

Dad frowned.

A perky brunette approached our table with a little too much bounce in her step, considering it wasn't yet ten in the morning. "Good morning, you two. Can I get you started with some drinks?"

"Coffee, please. Cream and sugar?" My dad remained completely oblivious to the stares we were getting. Either he had no idea, or he was trying to make the best of it. Likely, option B. He'd always been a peacekeeper. That's why it took him so long to get the balls to lock Mom away. Or maybe, in the end, locking her away had been his way of keeping the peace. I wouldn't know. No one had explained any of it to me. It was like when he'd told me we were moving. Simple, direct, with no room for argument. *"Stephen, I'm committing your mother to a mental hospital."*

My life with Dad was a series of simple statements.

"And you?" Donna smiled at me, her pen poised over the small pad of paper in her hand. She struck me as one of those really annoying people who love what it is they do for a living.

"I'll have a Mountain D—"

"Everyone! You're gonna burn. You're all gonna burn!"

I whipped my head around to the wild-eyed woman standing just inside the restaurant's front door. She was wearing a plain gray dress that reached her ankles, with sleeves that stretched all the way to her wrists, despite the fact that it was eighty-eight degrees outside. Around her neck she wore a small silver cross. In her hand she clutched a worn leather book. She didn't seem to be speaking to anyone in particular, and in return, most of the patrons simply hunched up their shoulders and tried to avoid eye contact with her.

The chain-smoking hostess approached her calmly, like this was a regular occurrence in her day. "Now, Martha, what have we talked about? You can't keep coming in here and disrupting people."

Martha didn't look like she gave a crap. She also looked like she pretty much lived on Planet Martha most of the time, with brief visits to the town of Whackadoo. When she spoke again, her tone remained every bit as embittered, but it was quieter, at least. "You'll all burn. You should be home on the Sabbath. Family and hearth. All of you."

By the pinched expression that was settling on the hostess's face, I could tell her patience was wearing thin. "Martha, we're trying to run a business here. If Dave sees you in here again causing trouble, you know what he'll do. He said he'd call Officer Bradley last time, and—"

"YOU'RE GONNA BURN!"

I was starting to like Martha.

The door opened, jostling the bell that hung above it, and a girl around my age rushed inside. Her shoulder-length hair was stark black, with streaks of cranberry and thin, plum-colored braids twisting all through it. She was dressed in small-town punk, with bold black-and-white-striped knee-high socks and beat-up military boots. Several safety pins were hooked along the hem of her short black skirt, and the tattered T-shirt she wore depicted a band I'd never heard of. Attached to the front of her shirt, clinging to her curves, was a button that read *Buttons Are for Dorks*. She definitely didn't look like a farmer's daughter.

She twisted one of her braids between two fingers in a way that was almost childlike. But there was nothing childish about the way she licked her lips or how she grazed the finger-nails of her left hand along the smooth skin of her thigh as she looked around the place. I took my time noticing.

When she saw Martha, she groaned. "Mom, come on. Come home. You can't keep doing this."

Martha gestured to the patrons dramatically with a sweep of her right arm. The hostess rolled her eyes. Something told me she'd heard this punch line so many times, she was just waiting for the joke to be over. "I have to warn them. I have to tell them."

The hostess spoke up again, her already-pinched face pinching even more in irritation. "Cara, I've had about enough of this. You've got to get her home and keep her there. Every Sunday, for crying out loud."

"I know, Mary. I'm sorry." The girl—Cara, I instantly memorized—turned back to her mom then, and my sympathy for her grew. It had to be hard to be the parent to your parent. It had to be hard to be the girl with the crazy mom. Especially when everyone in town seemed to know that was your lot in life. At least Dad had spared me that embarrassment.

Cara sighed, and then something sparked in her eyes. "Come on, Mom. What are you always saying we should do on the Sabbath? Stay home with our family, right?"

Her mom nodded eagerly. At last, someone was starting to listen to her. "Home and hearth. Family and home."

Cara tugged her sleeve and nodded at the door. "Well, come on, then. We're family. It's the Sabbath. Let's go home."

At first, Martha didn't move an inch. But then, with a distrusting gleam in her eyes and a furrowed brow, she edged toward the door, letting her daughter lead the way. As they exited, Cara glanced over her left shoulder, like she'd heard a sound or was checking to see if anyone else had anything to say about her crazy mother. When she did, our eyes met. I nodded a hello, and hoped she noticed, but I couldn't be certain. In seconds, she was gone. Off to take her mother home, on the Sabbath, like any good girl would.

chapter 2

After a full day of residing in Spencer, and a full three hours of lying awake in bed, I was beginning to worry that I might never sleep again. I was sure I wasn't the only restless person in our new house. I could hear my dad pacing down the hall, the sound only briefly accented by the ruffling of a newspaper. He was looking through the classifieds, if I had to put money on it.

Maybe my restlessness had something to do with the fact that my bedroom was stuffed so full of boxes that it felt more like some kid's cardboard fort than a place to sleep. Or maybe it was because every time I closed my eyes, I saw

Cara's nails scraping lightly against her thigh—shortly accompanied by Martha's words: *"YOU'RE GONNA BURN!"*

Whatever the reason, I was getting pretty sick of this bout of insomnia, and as far as I could tell, it had only just begun. Lucky me.

I wasn't sure why I kept thinking about Cara, anyway. She probably had a boyfriend. Girls like her always did. She was smokin' hot and a little bit badass. Her boyfriend was probably a biker or a thug or the leader of some gang. I wasn't anything so cool. My friends in Denver had all been nerds of one kind or another, but I couldn't really be defined by them. I wasn't a gamer, because I didn't own every system on the planet and beat every game the day it was released. I wasn't a book nerd, because I didn't enjoy the classics and had never met an author in person before. I wasn't a history geek, because the parts of history I enjoyed were the kinds of stories that qualified as useless trivia. I wasn't really anything at all.

And if I wasn't anything, how was I supposed to attract the attention of a girl who was probably looking for everything in a guy?

It didn't matter. That's what I told myself as I tossed and turned and tried not to think about the mysterious girl that occupied my thoughts. It didn't matter what she wanted or didn't want. I didn't even know her. For all I knew, she could be a real psycho. After all, didn't psycho run in the family?

I closed my eyes, drinking in the faint singsong of the crickets outside, blocking out any thoughts of Cara and her crazy mother, until finally, I slipped into the empty quiet of sleep.

Moments later, or maybe it was hours—with my alarm clock still lost in Fort Cardboard, I had no way of telling how long I'd dozed—I sat up, awakened by a noise. I listened closely, but there was nothing, just that eerie silence that comes with night in a small town. And then it hit me. It wasn't a sound that had woken me, but the lack of one. The crickets outside my window had gone abruptly quiet.

Stretching, I sat up and peered outside. Stars speckled the sky above, and my heart sank at the sight of them. In Denver, we couldn't see the stars in town because of the city lights. In Denver . . . well, a lot of things had been different.

I was about to lie back down when I noticed a strange silhouette standing on the sidewalk directly in front of the house. Whoever it was, they weren't moving at all, just standing there. I watched, curious, waiting for them to turn and walk away, but they didn't. And right as I became convinced that maybe it wasn't a person at all, but a tree or a mailbox that I'd forgotten about, the figure raised its arm and pointed directly at my window. It was definitely a guy.

My heart picked up its pace and I went straight into

attack mode. What the hell was that guy thinking? I threw on my jeans, T-shirt, and shoes, and moved through the house, quickly but quietly. All I wanted to do was scare the guy a little. Just a little warning to keep him from stalking around my place in the dark.

Not *my* place, I reminded myself. My grandmother's place. My temporary prison.

As I stepped outside, the screen door slapping closed behind me, I readied some choice words. My feet practically flew across the lawn to where the man had been standing, those words and more on my tongue, but there was no one there. The sidewalk was empty. A chill crawled up my spine, sending goose bumps all over my skin even in the oppressive heat of the midwestern summer. Behind me, all around the house, the crickets began to sing again.

A small, rectangular shadow near the sidewalk drew my attention, and I moved toward it to investigate. Plucking it from its spot in the grass, I realized I was holding a small leather book. Curiosity got the better of me and I tucked it in my back jeans pocket. For now, though, I had more pressing concerns.

The guy had been right here. Where the hell had he gone?

I looked up and down the street, and sure enough, the intruder was standing about four blocks up, watching me. Not running away, not looking to engage. Just standing there. Watching. Under the glow of the streetlight, I could see that his hair was white. From this distance, his eyes looked like two coals embedded in pale skin. He raised two fingers to his forehead in a salute before slowly turning and continuing on. My stomach muscles tightened as tension rose inside me. What was with the salute? Did he think we were buds after he'd stalked my window and seen me come after him? I didn't think so. And I was going to make damn sure he knew otherwise. I knew if I went back to bed, I wouldn't sleep—not unless I'd confronted this guy directly first. So I moved up the street, ready to teach him a lesson, but suddenly, he ducked in between two houses and disappeared.

"You need medication, dude. Seriously." My words were meant for the stranger, even though I knew he couldn't hear them.

The blocks were small—only four or five houses long— and there was only about a driveway's width between each house. As I passed the sixth house down, midway into the next block, a shout reverberated through the walls and windows. Someone was arguing. Not just arguing, but really fighting it out, in that way only family can. And try as I might not to eavesdrop, I found my footsteps slowing until I came to a stop on the sidewalk, wondering who else needed to have their prescription filled tonight.

"No good will come of fooling with the devil's instruments! Now hand them to me!"

I instantly recognized that shrill voice. I doubted there could be two voices in this town that sounded like that one. It could only be Martha. Still acting crazy, even though her audience was much smaller now than it had been in the Lakehouse Grill.

"Mom. No." The moment I realized that it was Cara speaking, my insides flexed. She sounded more than a little annoyed with her mother. What was crazy old Martha demanding that she hand over, anyway? The "devil's instruments"? Great. The girl I was attracted to was probably sacrificing goats or something.

"Where do you think you're going this late? It's the witching hour! It's not safe, Cara!"

The witching hour? Who said stuff like that?

Suddenly, the front door to the house flung open and Cara burst outside, throwing her hands in the air in absolute frustration. "Just leave me alone!"

I froze. She hadn't seen me yet, but when she did, she'd know I'd been eavesdropping. It wasn't like there was anything else I could have been doing outside their house in the middle of the night.

Cara lifted her head and I was caught for sure. Only—she didn't look all that surprised to see a strange boy standing there in the dark. I was starting to think that's just what people did around here. I was also starting to think that Cara was pissed, and I hoped it wasn't directed at me. She jabbed a thumb back at her house as she descended the steps. "So you heard all that, I suppose?"

"Just the part where she tried to save your soul and you basically told her to pop some pills." I smiled at her, hoping she'd laugh, hoping she'd get my weirdness and be okay with it. Then I realized how mean what I'd said might have sounded and my smile slipped. I shook my head in apology. "Sorry. I shouldn't joke about it. Not my business."

The corner of her mouth lifted in a small smile. She stepped onto the sidewalk next to me, and the streetlight glinted off the locket around her neck, held tight to her throat by a black satin ribbon. The locket was a silver heart, kept closed by what looked like wings. I tried to keep my gaze at eye level. Cara was about a foot shorter than me. So cute and petite that I easily could have picked her up and carried her around. I didn't, of course, because how creepy would that have been?

"It's okay. And yeah, you got the gist of it. How sad is it that my whole existence can be summed up by a stranger who overheard one argument with my mother?"

Stranger. For a moment, I'd completely forgotten about the stalker outside my window. But it didn't matter. This was a far better way to spend my time.

Stress was coming off Cara in waves, like heat. This wasn't exactly how I'd pictured meeting her, and I felt a little guilty about how excited I was when she was standing here hurting.

"I'm Stephen. You're Cara, right? I heard your mom say it." I gestured to the house with a nod and then smiled at Cara once again. "So now we're not strangers."

"Well, I'm definitely stranger than you. Bet on it." Her small smile spread into a full-on grin, lighting up her whole face. She looked so much prettier when she smiled. She tilted her head at me curiously. "You're new around here. How new?"

"New enough. My dad grew up here. He and I moved into my grandmother's house a block that way yesterday. Last night, really. Late." I had no idea why I kept adding details to my reply. It wasn't like she was quizzing me or anything. But the stupid just kept rolling out of my mouth like a red carpet. Inside, I was kicking myself.

"Sounds about right. Everybody who leaves comes back in the end. What are your thoughts on Spencer so far?"

For a moment, she seemed slightly guarded, waiting for my response. I couldn't tell if she wanted me to say I hated it or I liked it. I decided to be honest. They say the truth will set you free.

And nothing good had ever come my way on the heels of a lie.

"From what I've seen so far, it kind of sucks." She winced and I shrugged. Maybe that wasn't the right answer. But if she was sacrificing goats in her free time, did I really care about her opinion of me so much? "No offense."

She shrugged, too, and then nodded. If anything, she looked a little relieved to hear me say it. "None taken. I'm not the mayor. Hell, Spencer isn't even big enough to have a mayor. Just some stupid council. Where are you from, anyway? And how did you get stuck here?"

"I'm from Denver. And how I got stuck here is a long story, ending with my dad losing his job and my mom . . . well, staying behind, at least for now." I wasn't sure why I was telling her all this, especially outside her house in the dark, when we'd only just met. I just knew that I wanted to tell her whatever she wanted to hear about me. About anything.

She furrowed her brow sympathetically, and as my attention dropped briefly to her lips, I wondered where her dad was. I didn't dare ask. It seemed pushy to me, and I didn't want to push her. I wanted to kiss her. But only once we'd figured out that whole goat-sacrifice thing. "Can I tell your future?" she said.

"Well, *I* can, but only through the next school year. It

involves too many chores, not having my own car, and a C average, at best."

She flashed me a look that said she acknowledged what a smart-ass I could be, then held up a stack of Tarot cards. The edges of the cards were worn, softened with age and use. She said, "I meant with these."

I slipped my thumbs into my front jeans pockets and nodded, keeping a straight face. "Oh cool, the devil's instruments."

With a groan, she led me up onto the porch, where she knelt and then arranged her legs in a crisscross position. When I was in the second grade, my teacher, Mrs. Davis, told us this way of sitting was called crisscross applesauce. Mrs. Davis was obviously stupid.

The wooden planks that made up the porch were old to the point of dilapidation. It looked like they'd been painted a light-blue color once, but most of that had worn or peeled away with time and neglect. I could still see bits of the color on the edges of the porch, a hint at what a nice home this might have been, once upon a time.

I sat on my knees facing Cara and she handed me the deck. The cards were warm in my hands. Cara's warmth. Or maybe the fires of hell. I'd have to check with Martha to be certain. "Shuffle these and then cut them as much as you feel like."

I did as instructed, then handed the deck back to her.

Our fingers touched briefly, and I could have sworn I felt an electrical charge spark between us. But maybe that was just static. She took three cards from the top of the deck and laid them out side by side in front of her. "These three cards, from left to right, represent your past, your present, and your future. Got it?"

"Got it." I examined the cards. One looked like the grim reaper. The next looked like some kind of hairy demon. And the third looked like a mass suicide. I wasn't exactly filled with hope. "I'll be honest. Things look bleak."

Cara shook her head, a light smile dancing on her lips. "Things aren't always as they seem."

Our eyes met, and this time, for a too-brief moment, something definitely passed between us. I wasn't sure what it was, just that it *was*.

After our gaze broke, Cara went back to the cards. "So, in your past you have the Death card. I know it seems freaky, but that's actually a good position for that card. It means you've gone through a wrenching change that involved loss and a helpless inability to do anything about it. Probably your move to Spencer, or maybe your mom staying behind."

"Does it mention which box my alarm clock is in? Because I've been looking for it." I had to joke, because the whole thing with my mom and the move was just a bit too fresh for me to face.

"Come on, be serious." She shoved me playfully before tapping the card in the center. As she moved, I was reminded of her fingers scratching her thigh and had to bite the inside of my cheek just so I could focus on the task at hand. "In your present, you have the Devil."

I resisted the urge to ask her how much she knew about goat sacrifices.

"It's basically your wake-up call. You're hooked into something and may not even realize it. It could be the mind-set of being a victim, or something like that. Your thought processes and actions are currently holding you back. The Devil card here says that a terrible connection in your life right now is chaining you down from being who you truly are."

Who I truly am. Not a gamer. Not a book nerd. Not a history geek. Did this mean the devil was going to help me find out who I was? Looking at the cards and their weird cartoonish drawings, I doubted it.

"What's that? People are . . ." I pointed to the last card. It featured a building on fire. People were diving from the windows in a mad panic, screaming on their way down. Was that my future? I looked at Cara, hoping she'd shrug it off and tell me it was nothing. After all, she'd just said that things aren't always as they seem. "They don't look happy."

Neither did Cara. She bit her bottom lip and worry

creased her forehead. "This card is the Tower. The Tower card represents sudden change. To be honest, it's not the best card in the world to have in the future position. Having it here means that the decimation of some structure in your world will take place. It's also a pretty immediate thing. Whatever destruction is headed your way is headed your way now. Not in a year or two."

I stared at the card a moment longer before sighing. "Thanks. That's just great. I feel better about my life already."

"No problem." She ran her fingers lightly over the cards, keeping her eyes off me the entire time. I wondered why, but didn't want to ask. Mostly because she just might answer me.

Suddenly, someone behind me spoke. His voice was practically dripping with sarcasm. "Tell me that the Lovers didn't come up."

The look on Cara's face went from concerned to surprised to annoyed in about two heartbeats. She waved a hand at whoever was standing behind me and said, "Stephen, this is my twin brother, Devon."

As I turned to look at Cara's twin, I said a simple "Hey."

But the word fell flat. My heart beat solidly inside my chest. Because the boy I was looking at was the guy who'd been staring at my house less than an hour before.

chapter 3

Devon's sheared-short hair was so blond that it appeared white, in total contrast to his twin sister's. Like Cara, his eyes were dark, but that's where the similarities ended. His jawline was angular and smooth. It was amazing to me that these two could be twins—they were so different. But then, they were the first set of twins I'd ever met in person. Maybe twins being different from each other was more common than I realized.

Devon was dressed in black jeans, a gray T-shirt, and a thin, dark-gray hoodie with adornments that gave it a military look. That was fitting, because something about the way he stood, the way he carried himself, and the way he spoke made him seem commanding. I had a feeling Devon was used to being listened to.

My jaw tightened at the sight of him and I got to my feet. "You were staring at my window."

"Yeah."

"Why?"

"Does it matter?" We looked at each other for a good, long moment before Devon nodded to something, or maybe nothing at all, in the distance. "Come on. I want to show you something."

I hated not getting answers, but I tilted my head toward him anyway, curious. Listening, despite the vague understanding that I was *expected* to listen, which triggered my rebellious side. I hated expectations. "Show me what?"

Cara began picking up her Tarot cards with her right hand, shoving them angrily into a pile in her left. Her nail polish was chipped in several places, making her actions seem more frantic and violent than they really were. Without looking up at her brother, she said, "Do you have to do this every time? We were talking."

Devon slid his thumbs in his front pockets, staring at Cara until she finally looked up and met his eyes. Devon had willed her to. Such a small thing, but it seemed weird to me. Maybe it was because they were twins, and my closest encounter with twins until now had been Stanley Kubrick's creepy little girls in matching blue dresses, standing in the hallway of the Overlook Hotel. *"Come play with us, Stephen. Forever and ever . . ."*

Twins were weird. Or maybe I was just looking for weirdness. You know what they say: if you look hard enough for something, you're bound to find it.

After a moment of silence in which I tried to assure my wild imagination that they weren't using telepathy to communicate, Devon spoke. His voice was hushed, but just as commanding. "Every time. What's 'every time'? You don't even know him."

"I meant"—she glanced briefly at me before lowering her voice to something that sounded less angry—"that any time I'm talking to a guy, you get like this."

"Like what? How am I?" He barely gave her a second to answer, and when she responded by picking up the last of her cards in silence and standing, he grabbed her arm before she could walk away. "Seriously, how am I?"

With a glare, she shook him off. "Impossible. That's how you are."

"I kind of like the finality of that." The corners of his mouth were touched with the hint of a smile—one that didn't come through in his eyes. "Impossible."

A heaviness hung in the air between them—one I felt

obligated to ignore. This conversation was none of my business. Devon looked at me pointedly. "You coming or what?" I could tell by his tone that his patience was wearing thin.

Cara sighed. "Stephen, you don't have to go with him."

"But you can if you want. And I promise it'll be worth your while." He didn't look at his sister. His eyes were on me.

She groaned and rolled her eyes at her brother. "You are so annoying. What time will you be home?"

"Later." Devon shrugged casually with one shoulder.

Cara bit her bottom lip, glancing between her brother and me. "Dev—"

"*Later.*" His tone was more insistent, one not to be argued with.

Cara's eyes narrowed in a glare. She turned on her heel and walked through the front door, slamming it behind her.

I swallowed hard and became Mr. Obvious. "She's mad."

Devon's eyes followed her inside. He didn't look as concerned as I felt. "She'll get over it. Besides, what do you care? You just met."

He stepped down off the porch and I joined him, shaking my head. "I don't want to cause any trouble or make any enemies."

"What about friends?" He paused midstep and met my gaze. Then he cracked a smile and gave my sleeve a tug before continuing down the sidewalk. "Come on. I've got some people I want to introduce you to."

My eyes lingered on the door that Cara had just slammed, and I paused, contemplating my next move. If I left now, would Cara be mad at me later? Or was I too late to make a difference? Finally, I let my curiosity win out. I'd make it up to Cara the next time I saw her.

Devon and I walked along the grossly uneven sidewalk and passed the mansion I had seen from the car. Bright lights were flashing across the street from the gas station, and as we approached, I could see a car that had smashed into a telephone pole. The pole had given way and fallen on top of the car, denting its roof with the attached transformer. The windshield was smashed open completely. Two cops were on the scene. One was on his radio and the other was just kind of moseying around the car, looking important. The driver was still in the driver's seat, but the body was mostly covered up with a tarp. There was no ambulance in sight. I wondered if one was on the way from the city, or if the police hadn't even called one because it was too late.

"Holy shit. I think the driver is dead."

Devon just shrugged. "Spencer's going through a bad time right now."

My steps slowed momentarily. What an odd thing to say.

Devon grabbed my arm and pulled me away before the

cops noticed us. I couldn't believe how calm he was about the whole thing.

In silence, we made our way to the far end of town. It wasn't like Spencer was difficult to navigate—several of the streets were numbered, First through Fifth, and the streets that weren't numbered mostly fell in between—so I wasn't worried about getting lost. Once we hit Central Street, Devon steered us left, and when the street came to an end, he led me through some brush to a view of the reservoir— the one I'd seen online. The water was inky black under the night sky. I could see a few house lights peeking through a band of trees on the other side. A small peninsula jutted out from the land there. Old train tracks ran over a tall bridge and connected the peninsula to the land that made up Spencer. It was quite a scene. I bet my mom would have loved it.

It hurt to think pleasant things about my mom. Mostly because I was still kind of mad at her. If only she hadn't gotten sick. If only she could have gotten better sooner. Maybe we wouldn't be where we were now.

"It's nice, right? They call it the Holiday Reservoir. It's been here forever." The serene glass of the water shattered as Devon tossed a stone in, causing our reflections to ripple. He pointed to the area right below us. "But this section . . . this part right here . . . it's important. It has a dark history to people in Spencer."

I couldn't help thinking that this was how locals started telling urban legends to newcomers, but I was willing to play along for now. Just until the man with a hook for a hand became part of the storyline or that kid who hawked Life Cereal died by eating Pop Rocks and then drinking Diet Coke. Then I was definitely speaking up. "Oh yeah? Why's that?"

A breeze blew in across the water, ruffling our shirts. Devon's hair was cut so short that it didn't move. Neither did Devon. He was standing there, staring into the water below, looking like his mind was anywhere but with me in the present. "Years ago, there was a train wreck on the bridge over there. A few of the cars left the tracks and fell into the water. They were never recovered. Too heavy to lift, too expensive to afford. Spencer isn't exactly home to many rich people."

I raised an eyebrow at him. "What about the mansion?"

"That was William Spencer's—the guy that built this town. He was probably the only guy with real money who ever lived here. Most people in Spencer are broke or on their way to broke. Which is why, over the years, so many people have disposed of old appliances in this reservoir. It's like a weird kitchen graveyard down there." His eyes remained on the water, and I had to admit that I was more than a little curious as to where this story was going.

I peered down into the water, wondering if he saw something down there that I didn't.

"About six years ago, a boy named Bobby was swimming with a couple of friends. None of their parents knew, and all of them agreed that they'd change into dry clothes right after and keep it a secret. Their parents would have grounded them for a month for swimming out here without any adults around. It was a good plan. And they were having fun, y'know?" The corner of his mouth lifted in a smile, but it didn't last. "Then Bobby got the idea to dive down deep and explore the underwater graveyard. His friends begged him not to, but he promised it would be cool. So he went down. And he never came back up."

My stomach shriveled inside of me. Suddenly, the formerly serene water looked menacing. A boy had died here. Goose bumps rose on my arms, and I knew it wasn't because of the breeze.

Devon spoke again, but this time his voice was much softer. His eyes shimmered, mimicking the water below. "I dove in after a minute or so, worried he'd gotten snagged on a branch. I could hear Bobby pounding on something, but it took me a while to locate him. Sound is different underwater, y'know?"

I didn't know. I couldn't swim. But I nodded anyway, horrified that Devon had experienced this, and surprised that he was sharing it with me now. A person he didn't even know. It couldn't be easy.

"Once I found him, I realized he was trapped inside an old refrigerator. I tried, but I couldn't open the door. The water pressure was too much. I resurfaced and told Cara to go for help. I dove down again and pulled on the door as hard as I could, but I couldn't open it. I just couldn't. I wasn't strong enough. I tried again and again, but my lungs were burning and each time I dove down, I could only stay for a little while. I couldn't give up, though. He was my best friend." That last sentence came out in a strangled whisper.

I tried to think of something to say, some comforting words that might make him feel better or at least pull him out of the past, where his thoughts were clearly being held hostage. But nothing came to mind. Everything I could think of resembled a sappy Hallmark card. So I stood in silence, crossing my arms in front of me, waiting for Devon to get to the point. There had to be a reason he was telling a stranger such a deeply personal story.

"They pulled the refrigerator out with a crane. My dad wouldn't let me see them open it. But Bobby was dead. I knew that much." His tone became matter-of-fact. "My dad died last year, and my mom kind of went nuts because of it. So Cara's pretty much all I've got in this world. If you hurt her, I'll cut your balls off. Just so we're clear."

He met my eyes with his threat, and even in the darkness, I could see a sharp gleam there as he raised an eyebrow at me. "Are we, Stephen? Clear?"

So that's what this was about. He'd seen me and his sister hanging out and every protective nerve in his body had been set on high alert. Who could blame him? Especially with all he'd been through.

"Crystal, man. Crystal." And it was crystal clear. Hurt Cara and he'd hurt me. Not something I intended to do anyway, but I respected that he wanted me to know where we stood.

We watched the water for a bit, neither one of us speaking, until finally, I had to break the silence. "What time is it?"

"One thirty."

That explained the yawn I'd been fighting. "Does everyone in this town hang out so late?"

"Not everybody. Just everybody cool."

I couldn't escape the feeling that he was waiting for something, but I had no clue what that might be. If he was waiting for me to demonstrate my coolness, he was going to grow old in the process. "So who did you want me to meet?" I said.

"A group of guys I hang with." As if on cue, his phone buzzed in his pocket. He pulled it out and texted whoever it was, his face flashing ghostly white from the glow of the screen. I didn't have a cell phone. Somewhere around the hundredth hospital bill, my dad had told me he couldn't afford one for me anymore.

Devon hit send and looked up, noticing me staring. I said, "Nice phone."

He shrugged, slipping it back in his pocket. "Just one of the perks of a healthy life insurance policy."

What's a guy supposed to say to that? Before I could think of anything, he started walking back up Central to Water Street, toward the end of town where we both lived. As we approached First, Devon glanced at me with a smile. "Do you like old horror movies?"

Now he was speaking my language. I'd been a connoisseur of horror since my toddler years, thanks to my dad. Slasher flicks, suspense—I loved it all, from Hitchcock to Craven. "Almost exclusively. Why? You want to catch a flick?"

"That's exactly what I had in mind." He crossed the street to a brick building that had seen better days. Over the glass double doors hung an unlit marquee that read *Double Feature: Carrie and Night of the Living Dead*. Standing in front of the door, messing with the lock, was another boy our age. His hair was shaggy and black as pitch. Devon slapped him on the shoulder, ignoring the way his unexpected action made the boy jump. "Markus. This is Stephen."

Markus turned his attention to me briefly as I joined them under the marquee. "'Sup?"

I nodded my hello and tried to look cool, but really I wondered what the hell we were doing here. The theater was either out of business or closed for the night. And if Markus was doing what I thought he was doing to that lock, I wanted no part of it. Getting caught breaking and entering wasn't exactly going to keep my dad off my back for the rest of the summer.

Devon peered over Markus's shoulder. "Are we in yet?"

Markus pulled what looked like a bent paperclip from the keyhole. At the same time, he turned the knob, grinned back at Devon, and pushed the door open. "We were just waiting on you."

Devon offered an approving nod. "Text the boys."

Markus pulled out his phone and fired off a quick message. From where we stood, I could see the gas station and the lights of the cop car from earlier, but all other signs of the accident we'd seen were gone. Devon looked up and down the street, but he didn't seem too concerned about getting caught.

Ten very awkward minutes passed before a broad-shouldered guy rounded the corner. He looked like the kind of guy you might catch playing football on Friday night or riding a motorcycle. Following a few steps behind him was a smaller boy wearing glasses, his eyes downcast and his hands in his front pockets. Everything about the boy was skinny, including his jeans. He oozed quiet. With nods to Devon and then to Markus, but not even a glance in my direction, both boys headed inside the now-open door of the movie theater. I assumed we were going to follow them in, but Markus and Devon kept standing there, saying nothing, until finally two more boys walked up, each wearing a leather cuff on his left wrist. They were having a whispered conversation that I couldn't quite make out, and that conversation only got quieter as they passed us. Neither of them would look at me, either. They gave an almost-synchronized nod to Devon, smiled at Markus, and then kept right on walking.

Markus followed them in, but just as Devon was about to enter the building, I grabbed him by the shoulder, pulling him back. "Where are we going, exactly?"

"Where do you think? We can't watch a movie out here." Shaking my hand away, he entered the theater like he didn't care whether I came or not. I stood outside the open door for a good five minutes, debating whether I should go home or follow along. If I went home, I was a loser. If I went inside, I was a criminal. So basically, I had no choice.

The inside of the building smelled musty, like no one had cleaned the carpet in a decade, even though, I could now see, the theater was clearly open for business. The walls were covered in tacky, red-velvet-flocked wallpaper. The place looked more like some cheesy bordello than a movie theater. By the time I entered the lobby and closed the main door behind me, the last of Devon's as-yet-nameless friends were making their way into the theater through a red velvet curtain, with armloads of candy, soda, and popcorn. So much for introductions.

Devon was standing behind a glass case in the lobby, rifling through the remaining junk food. As I approached, he held up a yellow box. "Milk Duds?"

I shook my head, but he waved the box at me, rattling the candy inside. I took it with one more nervous glance at the door. "We shouldn't be in here."

"You can always leave." He raised an eyebrow at me. It was a question, a challenge. Was I cool enough to hang with Devon and his friends? Or was I going to puss out in the face of danger and run home to my daddy?

Devon moved through the curtain, again without waiting for my decision. Like brother, like sister. I hated to piss them both off in the same night, but if we got caught . . .

Screw it.

I grabbed a bag of Twizzlers and headed through the curtain.

In the shadow of the theater, I could make out Devon

sitting to the right of the biker guy and Mr. Glasses and Skinny Jeans. The other two boys were sitting off on their own. As I made my way to the empty seat beside Devon, I realized that Markus was missing and figured he must have been rigging up the projector. Sure enough, *Carrie* lit up on the screen in all of her 1976 glory just before Markus returned and took the seat to my right.

The book was way better, of course, but the movie version of *Carrie* was decent enough. And besides, I dug the main character. Carrie was an outcast, someone who was seriously bullied. Only Carrie had freaky mind powers—powers that she used to exact revenge on her tormentors. To any kid who had ever been picked on, Carrie was the stuff of heroes.

After Markus had changed the reel to *Night of the Living Dead*, I yawned and stretched and looked over at Devon. He was shoveling handfuls of popcorn into his mouth, his eyes locked on the black-and-white glory as the guy onscreen told his sister, "They're coming to get you, Barbara."

Devon had taken a chance, bringing me here tonight. He'd had no way of knowing if I was the kind of guy who would turn them in for breaking into the theater, or if I'd even come along at all. His friends might not have welcomed me, exactly, but it was pretty cool for him to take a chance like that.

"Hey, Devon." He glanced at me, a questioning look in his eyes. All I could think to say was, "Thanks."

He smiled, his lips slightly crooked, and shoved the half-eaten tub of popcorn into my hands. No further words were needed.

chapter

4

When he woke me up the next morning, my dad didn't mention the fact that I'd stumbled into the house just before dawn so he might not have noticed. But he also didn't offer to take me out for breakfast again or even give me time to shower. After a quick brush of my teeth and a swipe or two of deodorant, I got to work breaking down boxes that we'd emptied for recycling, still wearing my clothes from last night. I wanted to complain and go back to bed, but any complaints would have brought up questions about where I'd been, who I'd been with, and what I was doing out so late. I wasn't feeling up to answering any of that, so I kept my mouth shut and took my lack of sleep out on the boxes, stabbing them with my knife a few more times than was strictly necessary.

My dad had been way busier than I had in his unpacking efforts—every single one of his boxes was now in the pile I was making in the driveway. Either he was seriously anxious to settle in, or seriously nervous about what my grandmother would have to say if there was a mess. I was beginning to wonder if I was ever going to meet the old lady, or if she was just a twisted figment of my dad's imagination—kind of like Norman Bates's mom in *Psycho*.

My dad handed me a bottle of water and granted me a minute's rest while he headed back inside, so I sat on the hood of the Beetle and took a swig. That's when I noticed the four members of the Spencer tanning club—the teens from outside the Lakehouse Grill—strolling up the sidewalk.

I was really hoping they wouldn't notice me—that they'd just keep walking. In fact, if I'd believed in a god, I even might have prayed about it. It was embarrassing enough to be seen with the Beetle once, but at least last time they'd been on the way out. I'd been picked on enough times at my old school to know that rich kids didn't like us poor kids, and this beat-up Beetle made it pretty clear we were poor. I wasn't in the mood to be picked on by anyone here. Not with everything else I had to deal with.

Racquetball Boy smiled at me as they made their way to

the end of my grandmother's driveway, and all four of them stopped, looking from the boxes to the Beetle to me.

Shit.

One of the guys in the group was holding a Frisbee, but there was nothing ultimate about it as far as I could see. Racquetball said, "Hey. I'm Lane. This is Casey, Mike, and Holly. You just move in or something?"

A genius Lane was not. Trying hard not to focus on the fact that this guy's parents had named him after a narrow road, I nodded in response, wondering where the hell that narrow road might lead. Not an educational institution. Probably a kegger or maybe an ice cream social. "Yeah. From Denver. I'm Stephen, by the way."

Holly bounced forward in the most obnoxious way possible, and I immediately placed a bet with myself that she was a cheerleader. Not that I had anything against cheerleaders, in theory. And it wasn't that I didn't appreciate the jiggle. But something about her peppy smile made me want to hurry back to whatever chores my dad had in mind. She was definitely a morning person. "We were heading to the park. Would you like to join us?"

I held up my hands and shrugged as sheepishly as I could manage. "Can't. Gotta unpack today. But it was nice meeting you guys."

Lane nodded. Even though he was still smiling, I could

see the disappointment in his eyes. "Cool. Well, maybe we'll see you around later."

"Yeah, maybe." I sincerely hoped not. They were pretty annoying. I couldn't exactly put my finger on why. They were just . . . annoying. Like some people are.

They continued down the sidewalk a ways before crossing the street. My dad joined me beside the Beetle, a bit too chipper for my tastes. "Are those the guys you were out with last night? Making new friends?"

"Not exactly." I was hoping that would be all the answer he needed, but as he stared at me, it became pretty clear he wanted me to elaborate. Oh sure, *now* he wanted to talk about things. I sighed. "They're not friend material, Dad. Not for me."

"You should be more open-minded, Stephen. It can be difficult to fit in and meet new people, especially in a town this size. And who knows how long we're going to be here. Maybe give them a chance." He stood there looking at me, waiting for some sign that his wisdom was sinking in. The only response I gave him was to pull the small leather book from my back pocket, the one I'd found on the sidewalk last night, and ruffle its pages with my thumb. Finally, he gave up and walked back inside.

As if he had any right to offer me fatherly advice. After all he was putting me through.

I turned the book over in my hand, examining it closely. In the dark, I'd thought it might be somebody's Bible or something. Now I could see the cover was red leather, but so worn that it looked almost brown. The material felt soft in my palm as I peeled back one cover and let the pages flip quickly between my fingers. It turned out it wasn't a Bible at all, but a crazy sketchbook or somebody's journal. Somebody who apparently had a thing for birds—there were scratchy drawings of wings on almost every page, as well as words. It occurred to me that this might belong to Devon, since he was the one who'd been standing outside my house last night, and I'd found the journal right where he'd been. As soon as I had the thought, I wanted to see what was in the journal more than ever—but I also felt like I was invading his privacy somehow. I decided I'd give the journal back to Devon the second he asked for it. But if he didn't ask for it . . . I shoved it in my pocket, emptied my bottle of water, and retrieved my knife from where I'd dropped it in the driveway.

I'd just made it to my bedroom to grab more boxes and then maybe take a much-needed nap when a voice from behind me stopped me cold.

"That doesn't go there, Harold!"

It was an older woman's voice, coming from the open front door of the house that I was supposed to be viewing as home. It was weird to hear my dad called Harold, as he had gone by "Rollie" for as long as I could remember. It had to be her, Dad's mom, my grandmother. Who else would be yelling at him like he was a child? I turned my head to get a look at her.

The woman standing at the front door wore a pinched expression on her face, and judging from her frown lines I guessed that that was pretty much the only expression she ever wore, no matter what her mood was. Her eyelids were painted in thick blue, her lips lined in a color that was distinctly darker than the rest of her mouth. Her hair was pulled back tightly from her face and carefully wound into a bun that sat atop her head. She was dressed in powder-blue polyester slacks, with a silky top that had more flowers than I'd ever seen in one place before. Her blouse was buttoned all the way to her neck, but the buttons were hidden by a large ruffle. This had probably been stylish fifty years ago.

The line of her mouth struck me as very familiar. It only took me a moment to identify it as my dad's mouth—or to realize that my grandmother also had my dad's nose. I guess it was the other way around, really. He didn't have her eyes, though. I did.

As those eyes fell on me, the left corner of her mouth twitched. Not a smile. Not even the hint of one. Just a twitch. Like a bad taste had settled in her mouth or something. She didn't say anything to me, but instead spoke to my dad as she looked at me through a veil of disapproval. "I won't put up with messes, Harold. The boy looks unkempt. Does he keep his room clean?"

If I'd ever wanted to know what it felt like to be the Invisible Man, I was getting a good taste of it then. But I wasn't about to be ignored. You could do whatever you wanted to me, but I was a person. Don't ignore me. Don't pretend like I don't exist, when I'm standing directly in front of you. "Hi. I'm Stephen. You must be my grandmother. Nice to meet you."

She looked me up and down with a sour purse of her lips, then went back to pretending I wasn't there at all. "He looks dirty. Didn't you and that wife of yours teach him anything?"

"No, really. It's very nice to meet you." It was ridiculous the way she went on as if I hadn't just spoken to her. Like maybe if she ignored my presence long enough, I'd evaporate into thin air. Maybe that's what she wanted. But it wasn't what she was getting. We were here now. I was here. Like it or not, we were stuck together.

She snorted in derision, as if she'd heard my inner observation and didn't like it any more than I did. "Clean up my yard, Harold. I want everything looking its usual way by this afternoon."

She didn't wait for a response. She simply went back to

her room and closed the door with a loud click—not a slam, exactly. Nothing so noisy. Just enough of a sound to make her displeasure known. Once she'd gone, I grunted. "Wow. I want to be her when I grow up."

My dad shot me a look that was either telling me to watch my mouth or, more likely, pleading with me not to be like his mother in even the smallest sense. I said, "Sarcasm, Dad. Don't worry. I'm starting to understand why you left this place and stayed away for so long."

"Your grandmother and I fail to see eye to eye on many things. But let's just try and make the best of a bad situation. She may warm up to you in time."

"Yeah. Maybe." That was what I said. But what I thought was, "The hell she will."

The fact was, there was no pleasing some people because some people didn't ever want to be pleased. I got a gnawing feeling in my stomach that said my grandmother belonged to that club. But screw her. I had had a life before her and I'd have a life after. Only six months stood between me and the age of majority, and if my dad didn't move us out of her crappy house before then, I was gone—off to college, or anywhere else far away from my family and their screwed-up problems. Away from my bitter grandmother and her pursed lips and whatever ideas she'd already made up her mind about when it came to me.

My dad went outside to clear stuff from the front lawn, and with a sigh, I turned back to the task at hand. The boxes in my room weren't going to break themselves down.

"Harold." She'd stuck her head out her door again, but just long enough to bark an order disguised as a request. "It would be nice, since I'm letting you live here rent-free if you and the boy could do some maintenance around the house to repay me. You can start by scraping the old caulk from the windows and redoing it. Don't make a mess, now."

She disappeared again before he could say anything. The look in his eyes as he dropped another stack of cardboard in the recycling pile was one I hated to see. It was a look of defeat.

chapter 5

The outside of Tom's Hardware was plain and painted cinder-block gray, with the name written out on the simplest of signs hanging over the glass front door. The inside was cramped, overstuffed with the kinds of manly-man things that I largely didn't give a crap about. Buckets of various-sized screws were everywhere. And it had this weird hardware-store smell, like grease and loneliness. But that didn't seem to bother the four old men who were crowded around the cash register, talking to the old man standing behind the counter—presumably Tom.

This group of old men looked vaguely similar to the one

that had been outside the gas station when we'd first arrived in town, but there was no way I could pick either group out of a lineup. They were all old. They were all men. One of these guys had a kind of mustache or something. At this point, all I knew was that we'd been working on my grandmother's stupid windows for a week now, and my dad had sent me here to buy more caulk. I had snickered like an idiot when he told me to buy the big tube.

Who knew that a week could stretch into an eternity when you were doing everything at someone else's bidding, for someone else's benefit? I did. Now I did, anyway. Every day of my new life had begun with scrambled eggs and luke-warm showers, and every night had ended with me lying on my bed, exhausted but unable to sleep. When my grand-mother wasn't at home coming up with mile-long to-do lists for Dad and me, Dad was on the internet, scouring every job site he could find. When I told him he'd better not be looking for any jobs in Spencer, he'd said there weren't any jobs in Spencer to find, anyway.

Now, as I moved through the aisles, searching for a row of pointy-ended white tubular things, the conversation from the cash register floated over the tops of the shelves to my ears. It's not like I meant to eavesdrop. It's not like I really gave two craps about old-men gossip. But it was there and so was I, and I listened in an offhand way.

"I told Bert that car wouldn't make it another week. Damn engine hadda blown head gasket. Only an idiot woulda kept driving it." The way he said "idiot" made it sound more like "idjit." I rolled my eyes.

A second old man jumped to Bert's defense with a nasal tone. "A man's gotta get to work."

The first old man snorted. "He couldn't walk to the Grill? Hell, I used to hoof it three miles to work before I got the Caddy. He only lived a mile outsidah town."

A third old man chimed in, his voice so mechanical that I wondered if he was speaking through one of those devices they attach to your neck after throat cancer surgery. "Speakin' o' the Grill. That Mary's a fine-lookin' woman. She single yet?"

"Still married to that Bob Gunderman fella. He's a hunter with a bad temper, Bob. So if you're lookin' t'flirt with Mary, you best stick to lunch at the Grill." I moved down another aisle, wondering just where the stupid caulk was kept anyway. Narnia?

"Just don't go on Sunday." At this, the entire group guffawed. I spied the shelf of caulk tubes at last, right at the end of the aisle I was in. I picked one up and scanned the label— not that I had any idea what to look for besides *big*.

"That Martha is one crazy ol' bat, ain't she?" Bert's defender lowered his voice when he spoke of Martha. I hoped he'd done so because he was ashamed to be talking about someone behind their back, but I doubted it. "And those kids of hers. Must be hard not having their daddy around to help raise 'em right."

The guy with the robotic voice said, "Now it won't do no good to speak ill of the dead, Frank."

Frank huffed a little. "Not speakin' ill, just sayin' the man's dead."

"Dead? Well. Seems that brings us full circle—all the way to Bert's car." They all laughed at the nasal man's quip—all, of course, but for the first old man, who seemed downright irritated.

As I rounded the corner and headed to the cash register, they all fell silent. I didn't even get a chance to set the two tubes of caulk I'd grabbed on the counter before the one I thought was Tom said, "Eight dollars even."

I paid the man and took my receipt before heading out the door, hoping that I'd never have to go back inside Tom's Hardware ever again.

A few hours later, the tubes were all but empty, and I was sick of being stuck on a ladder doing work for a woman who clearly loathed my very existence for no apparent reason. Dad had put me in charge of washing the windows after we'd finished caulking them, and then had taken a ridiculous amount of time to stand in the yard and admire my work. By "admire," of course, I meant "critique." Which was such an incredible help.

By "help," of course, I meant "pain in the ass."

Screw it. If I took the time to define every term and definition my father dealt in, I'd end up inventing a whole other language. One called Bullshit.

He'd finally gone inside and left me alone for the last one. I think he could tell my temper was running short.

"Hey." As I ran the wet sponge over the final windowpane, a familiar voice reached my ears—one I hadn't been expecting. I turned around to see Cara standing at the end of my driveway, a backpack slung over one shoulder. She was wearing another short skirt today—this one red plaid—and black thigh-high stockings with satin bows on the top. I could have told her that she didn't need the bows to draw attention to her thighs, but didn't want to risk getting slapped. Instead, I moved my eyes up the length of her body, appreciating every inch. She wore dozens of bracelets on each wrist—some simple rubber things, some leather straps with pyramid studs. The T-shirt that I was envying for clinging so closely to her curves had a drawing of some kind of sea creature with a unicorn horn. Framing the picture were the words *Narwhals Are Sexy*.

I didn't know what a narwhal was, but I lingered on "sexy" for a moment before moving up to her eyes, lined in thick black. Her hair contained purple and blue falls and featured several barrettes that looked like grinning skulls. And when she smiled, I noticed how shiny her lip gloss was. Like glass, only more inviting. Maybe like a mirror. Whatever. I wasn't a poet, I just wanted to kiss her. Preferably when no one else was around and she was feeling frisky.

My dad chose that moment to step outside, carrying a plate of turkey sandwiches. But he couldn't resist the chance to criticize my window-washing abilities one more time. Like it was a thing I'd put on my résumé someday. "Is that window streaked? You shouldn't leave streaks, Stephen. They'll drive your grandmother crazy."

Rolling my eyes, I stepped down from the ladder and shoved the sponge into his free hand before joining Cara on the sidewalk. My dad blinked, taking in the situation for a moment before realization hit his eyes. I could tell he had a million questions about who the strange hot girl was and why she was standing in front of our new home. To his credit, he kept his mouth shut. Also to his credit, he didn't look at Cara in that pervy way that old guys sometimes look at younger punk girls.

Cara raised her eyebrows, a small smile touching her shiny lips, and said, only to me, "You busy?"

Without a word, and pretending that he wasn't totally eavesdropping—which he totally was—my dad approached the ladder and adjusted it. Needlessly. We both knew what he was doing, and that it had nothing to do with the windows and everything to do with the sudden appearance of Cara, but neither one of us pointed out that obvious fact. Instead, I tried to pretend that my dad didn't exist. "Kind of. What's up?"

"I was thinking of heading to the Playground and doing some charcoal rubbings. Wanna join me?" Her eyes flicked from me to my dad. I was pretty sure if it were up to him, I would be going nowhere today. Not only because he needed my help, either. All week, he'd been treating me like I was being punished for something, and he just wouldn't say what. Probably all the mouthing off I'd done. But what did he expect? I had to do something to liven things up. He kind of had it coming.

To my immense surprise, my dad just smiled and offered a nod, telling me to go ahead. Maybe even Dad understood that when a hot girl beckons you somewhere, you don't question it, you just go.

Drying my palms on my jeans, I smiled at Cara. "Let's go."

"Home by dinnertime, Stephen." Glancing back, I could see a mixture of feelings in my dad's eyes. Mostly hope, but also a tinge of concern. It might've been because Cara looked different than the girls he was used to seeing me with back in Colorado.

We walked a block down Fourth to Pine and took that street all the way to the northern end of town, past the movie theater and several small boxy houses of varying drab colors. I was glad that she wasn't feeling too chatty, because I wasn't exactly sure what I could talk about without revealing myself to be a loser. And besides, I was still kind of worried about the fact that I had ditched her a week ago. She might have been pissed. Around her neck I spied the locket she'd been wearing the first time I saw her, but I didn't linger. Mostly because I was trying to act casual about the way I was checking her out.

Just as we were about to run out of street, I cleared my throat and said, "So, what exactly are we rubbing at the playground?"

Cara grinned. "Don't get your hopes up just yet. The Playground is what locals call the cemetery. We're going to do some charcoal rubbings of tombstones. Have you ever done grave rubbings before?"

I shook my head and her smile softened. "It's easier than you might think, and the end result is really cool. I have a few hanging up in my bedroom. You'll love it, I promise."

My stomach shrank a little in disappointment that the

rubbing we were doing involved charcoal, but I was pretty geeked about visiting the cemetery. Also about the fact that she'd mentioned her bedroom, because it gave me a chance to picture her in bed. Possibly naked.

At the edge of town, Cara led me down a long dirt road, lined with silver maple trees. Their jagged, pointed leaves shuffled in the wind. The only other sound was that of some birds singing a mournful whistle. We passed an old shed on the right and came to a small hill—sitting atop it was a tombstone bearing the name of William Spencer, the town's founder. There was no gate identifying the beginning of the cemetery. It was just part of the town, as death was just a part of life.

The cemetery had an abandoned feel to it, and I wondered whether they were still burying people here, or if this was full and forgotten. "Why the 'Playground'? Kind of a weird thing to call a cemetery, isn't it?"

Cara shrugged as she led me past the hill and down the dirt road. To our right were graves. To our left was the reservoir, behind a thin row of trees. "It's a pretty regular hangout for Spencer kids, so the nickname just seemed natural, I guess. I don't know. People have been calling it the Playground since the eighties or something."

"That long?" I joked.

"I know, right? Practically prehistoric."

The road ended at a cliff, overlooking the water. When we reached it, Cara steered us right, to some of the oldest-looking tombstones in the cemetery. Her eyes scanned them, like she was choosing the perfect stone for her project. Finally, she settled on a small, white one featuring a carving of a lamb. On sight, I knew it to be the headstone of a kid.

When I was about ten years old, my dad volunteered for this community clean-up crew. He was assigned to help rake away the dead leaves in the fall, and one day, when his crew was cleaning the Fairmount Cemetery, he brought me along to help. I came across all these carvings of lambs on the smaller stones in the oldest part of the cemetery. When I asked Dad about them, he said the Victorians loved their symbolism, and a lamb was the symbol of choice when it came to gravestones for children. It represented innocence.

Cara got on her knees and unzipped her backpack. I looked around at the cemetery for a minute before joining her. "So what got you into grave rubbings?" I asked.

"My dad taught me. Plus, I've just always had a fascination with death and the weird rituals that people practice around it." She laid her supplies out neatly on the ground before meeting my eyes. When she looked at me, my heart jumped into my throat for a second. If it was possible, she was even prettier here, surrounded by all these reminders of people who had once lived. "Gravestone rubbing is really easy. You just brush the stone free of dirt, wash it down with a spray bottle and rag, then tape the rice paper in place and rub the stone over with charcoal. The key is to be incredibly gentle, or else you can damage the stone."

I blinked in confusion for a few seconds, then finally realized what she was saying. She expected me to do a rubbing, too. "I'm . . . not an artist, exactly."

"Don't be silly. Everyone's an artist. You probably just haven't found your medium yet." She smiled brightly and pointed at the small stone next to the one she had chosen. This one marked the grave of two children together. Judging from the engraving, they'd died on the same date.

After watching her for a while, I hesitantly reached for a soft bristle brush to clean dirt from the letters on the stone. Grabbing the spray bottle, I squirted several pumps of water onto the granite and gently wiped it clean with the cotton cloth, careful to mimic her every move. Then I sat back, scanning the stone for any sign of dirt, and waited for it to dry.

Cara glanced over at me. I couldn't tell if she was checking my progress, or checking me out, or both. "This is nice. Usually I'm up here all alone."

"I'm glad you invited me." And I *was* glad. Cara's company was easy and natural. I still wasn't sure if she'd been sacrificing goats or not, but that was mattering less and less.

I taped a sheet of rice paper to the stone and reached for a charcoal pencil, my fingers brushing Cara's as she did the same. We both broke into stupid grins.

The cemetery had grown quiet. The breeze had settled, leaving us sweltering in the summer heat. The mourning doves had silenced their song. Our only company was the sun, which had risen to its highest point in the sky, warming my shoulders as I dragged the charcoal across the paper, documenting the inscription on the gravestone one section at a time. In a way, we were preserving history. I liked that. The past had to be remembered. Otherwise, all we had was the present. And the present largely sucked.

I stood and stretched for a moment, brushing dirt from my jeans. A slight sheen caught my attention, and I followed it two graves down the row to a small, round-topped stone. Beside this grave lay a long, black feather, so shiny it almost seemed metallic, unreal. I turned it over in the sunlight. One side was so glossy it was almost reflective; the other was dull, barely picking up the light at all. Immediately, my thoughts turned to the journal I'd found—the one I was still calling Devon's journal in my head, even though Devon had yet to come asking for it. The journal had been sitting in the top drawer of my nightstand for the past week, calling my name. I'd still only flipped through it briefly the once, but several pages had contained sketches of wings. Wings made of feathers that looked a lot like this one.

Cara said, "It's probably a crow's feather. They fly around here a lot."

I looked up at the empty sky and back to Cara, who was chewing her bottom lip, her eyes locked on the feather. Softly—almost whispering—she said, "Did you know that a group of crows is called a murder? A murder of crows. I've always found that interesting."

I dropped the feather to the ground and shrugged. "You're right. Probably just a crow."

But it wasn't a crow's feather. And Cara knew it.

She shook her head, forcing out a small laugh that I didn't quite buy. "Well, it might be something else, if you believe the old people in town."

"Oh yeah? Like what?"

She kept trying to play her words off casually, but something wasn't sticking. "Oh, I don't know. There are these stories that go back since before Spencer was even officially a town. Ridiculous stories, about these giant flying creatures. People call them the Winged Ones—say they've been appearing before big tragedies since the town's first settlers arrived."

"So they're like an omen? With feathers?" A small chuckle escaped me, but I caught it as soon as I saw the look on her face.

"Not really. I mean . . ." She dropped her gaze to the ground between us, an expression of reluctance settling into her features. Reluctance to reveal something so strange about her town, I was guessing. Telling it to an outsider like me must have felt like revealing something embarrassing about herself. "Well, if you believe what people say, the Winged Ones *eat* people. They show up during the bad times—which, yeah, I guess is like an omen or something—only it's more than that. It's like they bring the bad times with them. People believe if you appease the Winged Ones with a sacrifice, they'll go away again. Poof. Bad times over."

I shook my head. Who would believe in something like that? In this day and age?

"That's crazy."

"That's Spencer."

And just like, she went back to her grave rubbing.

From the corner of my eye, I watched Cara's skilled fingers move over her paper in a blur. I returned to my spot at the stone I'd been working on, trying to shake off the weird folktale she'd told me. I said, "So, I take it you're not pissed about me ditching you the other night?"

"What made you think I'd be mad? I'm used to people choosing Devon over me."

My heart sank. What a horrible way to feel. I hated that I'd been the one to make her feel it this time. I said, "Just so you know, I didn't . . . I wouldn't . . . I mean, just because I was curious about what he had to show me doesn't mean I'd pick time with your brother over time with you."

"But you did." She paused briefly and met my eyes. The hurt in hers was evident.

My chest grew tight with guilt. "I'm sorry."

"It's okay, Stephen. You just wanna make friends here. I get it." She smiled mischievously. "But just so *you* know . . . I'm a way better kisser than he is."

Instinctively, my eyes dropped to her lips, as my own turned up in a hopeful smirk. "Prove it."

"If you're lucky." She winked at me and I felt my heartbeat speed up. I didn't go back to my charcoal, half hoping that this flirting meant she'd rather make out a little instead. When she picked up her own charcoal again, I let out a little sigh of disappointment. Then I pulled myself together.

"So are you and Devon close? I've heard that about twins."

"We used to be." She paused and took in a shaking breath. "Our dad died a year ago, and ever since then, things have been different. Mom checked out of our lives and into her Bible, leaving me and Devon to fend for ourselves. Devon couldn't take it, I guess, so he pulled away from pretty much everyone. Even me."

She smiled weakly, as if this didn't bother her. She was

a terrible liar. I dropped the subject, but couldn't help marveling at her strength, putting on a happy face when she was going through so much. We exchanged a silent conversation with a glance, and then she went back to work, signaling that I should do the same.

For several minutes, we worked quietly. Full, dark clouds rolled in overhead, the perfect backdrop to our endeavor. Cara finished up with the stone she was rubbing and began picking pieces of tape from the edges, freeing her artwork. It had turned out perfectly, with each bit of the carving marked in an exact charcoal replica on the paper. Much better than mine, which I'd smudged in several places, marring my creation with random black thumbprints. Cara rolled both rubbings up carefully and slipped them inside a plastic tube from her backpack.

A white Crown Victoria pulled slowly into the cemetery, stopping in the road down by William Spencer's grave. Blue and red lights lined the roof but remained unlit. Painted on the side of the car, in electric blue, was *Spencer Police*. Even though it had been a week, my first thought was that someone had blabbed about my involvement in the theater break-in—that we'd overlooked a security camera or something. I was going to jail. If my dad didn't kill me first.

Apparently, Cara was dealing with similar fears. She swore under her breath and started gathering up the supplies as quickly as she could. "Come on, we'd better get out of here. Officer Bradley isn't a big fan of art . . . or of me."

Cara stuffed her supplies into her backpack and bolted for the tree line on the far side of the cemetery. I sprinted after her, not bothering to question why we were running. In Denver, cops plus teenagers generally didn't equal fun, and I wasn't about to hang around and find out if things were different in Spencer. Up ahead, Cara had disappeared into the surrounding woods. I had no idea where we were going, but I kept on running, my chest burning, trying to keep up with her lightning-fast pace. Then the skies opened up and rain poured down on us, making my skin slick, soaking my hair, my clothes. Even with the cover of the trees, I was drenched in seconds.

But I kept running, going, chasing after Cara, and feeling free.

It felt good. *I* felt good. Better, in fact, than I had in a long time.

At last, I rounded a moss-covered oak and came to the clearing where Cara had paused to rest. I stumbled to a stop beside her, nearly falling. She reached out a hand and steadied me, then placed the same hand to her chest to calm her breathing. I leaned against the oak, watching her, trying to catch my breath in the pouring rain. I looked up briefly and felt like I was drowning.

Cara leaned against the tree, too, her chest rising and falling in deep, panting breaths. Curves straining against dripping wet clothes. She closed her eyes and turned her face upward, letting the streams of water brush her hair back from her face.

It was the most beautiful sight I had ever seen.

Without thought, without worry, without any of the possible repercussions winding through my mind, I leaned in and pressed my lips against hers. My eager hands found her waist and pulled her to me, wanting her close. There was a soft thump as her backpack fell to the ground at our feet, but I barely noticed it. All I heard was the thunder of my heart, the still-falling rain, and the soft *mmm* Cara made when I kissed her.

I pulled away slowly. I whispered, "I'm sorry."

"I'm not." She smiled up at me, her breath hot on my neck. We were standing so close that I could feel the heat of her flushed skin against mine, but neither of us moved. Neither of us spoke. The rain lightened up until it was barely drizzling. I watched water stream from the tips of Cara's hair and down her face. I was about to tell her she was beautiful, when she kissed me.

chapter 6

My dad didn't ask about the strange girl I'd never mentioned, but over the next few days, I caught him eyeing me
like he was trying to figure out who this boy was who looked
a lot like his son.

We'd finished caulking the windows, but my grandmother had decided that her toolshed needed to be scraped
and repainted. So Dad and I scraped and sanded, patched
and primed, and mostly pretended that we were cool with
each other when we weren't—not really. Life in Spencer was
wearing him down. And the bills for my mom had finally
found us here—my grandmother had left the first one

pinned up on the refrigerator for us to find after dinner one night. Just about the only time I could relax around my dad was when he had his nose in the paper or his laptop open, searching so desperately for employment that it was starting to seem might never come.

I spent as much time as possible in my room and away from him, wondering how Cara was and if she'd been thinking much about me. I hadn't seen her or Devon around during my errands into town, and I kept stopping just shy of knocking on their door. I was starting to think the night at the movie theater had been some sort of test, and I'd failed. And I didn't want Cara to think I was stalking her or something. Things would have been a lot easier if I'd had a cell phone.

Dad peered down at me from his place on the ladder and cleared his throat. "I talked to your mom this afternoon. She said she still hasn't heard from you since the move."

"I was going to call her last night but Grandma was on the phone."

"Uh-huh. Sure. Just call her, Stephen. She's your mother, for crying out loud."

She's not my mother, I thought. Not anymore.

But I just nodded and passed him the paintbrush.

Once we finished putting on the second coat of Soul-Sucking Gray—which might not have been the official shade, but who from Sherwin-Williams was going to stop me from calling it that?—I headed inside to grab a quick shower. I'd hardly made it ten feet before the sudden, powerful urge to call my mother swept over me. Before I knew it, I had the receiver in my hand and two numbers dialed. The truth was, my dad was right. The truth was, I missed her. I should let her know that I was okay, the move went fine, that there were some parts of my new home I was actually enjoying and I felt guilty because she wasn't here to see that. She was my *mom*. Crazy or not, she had to be scared being shut up in a strange place with no family around. She probably missed us, missed me. And my refusal to pick up the phone until now couldn't be helping matters.

On the other hand . . .

I slammed the receiver back down with a shaky breath. As selfish as it sounded, it didn't matter what she was probably feeling at the moment. I was still hurt and angry and not ready to hear her voice. I knew it was irrational, but I couldn't help it.

I went to bed that night without ever taking a shower and with a load of guilt weighing down my thoughts. In an effort to distract myself, I devoured every page of that small leather book—which *definitely* turned out to be Devon's journal. He'd signed his name on some of the sketches and poems, as if he'd *meant* for someone other than himself to read it all. At least, that's how I justified what I was doing.

A few pages in, I found a scratchy-looking sketch of a bird's wing, drawn in heavy black lines that seemed so raw, so immediate, it was as if Devon had been driven to get the image out of his mind and onto the page as quickly as he could. Almost as if by drawing it, he could remove it from his thoughts—purge himself of the image. The wing dipped onto the opposite page, pointing to a few lines of poetry that Devon had attributed to someone named Michael R. Collings. The poem spoke of "winged shadows in clefts of wailing yews."

Not that I had any idea what a yew was.

I flipped to the next page. A more carefully drawn sketch occupied much of the left side, as if Devon had taken his time with this one, maybe reveled in what it was that he'd been drawing. Maybe this was an image he wanted etched into his thoughts as well as onto the page. Who could say but Devon? All I knew was that whoever had drawn this large, winged creature attacking a train car had taken his time doing it. The detail was incredible. Tiny, horrified faces peered out of the car windows, mouths agape in screams as the car left the tracks. Water swirled in the reservoir below. Each feather on the creature's wing was drawn in intricate detail. There were no words on this page. The picture was enough. The next page, however, contained only words—a few lines

Devon had credited to someone named Lynn Samsel. I wondered how deeply they had spoken to him:

No one I know talks to crows the way I do.
Probably no one listens to them either.

"Probably not, my friend," I muttered.

I turned the pages, past more drawings and more poetry and song lyrics. I stopped on a sketch that grabbed my attention and refused to release its grip. It was of a building on fire. Perched on top of the building was another large, winged creature. In its beak was a lit match.

I closed the journal and dropped it back into the drawer of my nightstand before stretching with a good yawn. All in all, it was a cool piece of fiction, and even though it might be wrong to do so, I was planning on keeping it.

I drifted off with images of giant black wings in my mind, but I didn't sleep for long. A tapping sound woke me. Knuckles on glass. When I pulled back my newly hung curtains, it was to find Devon himself, beckoning me with a crooked finger. I smiled and nodded, but inside, my stomach twisted in a knot. Surely he didn't know about the journal. He couldn't. I released the fabric, letting it fall back into place, and debated my options.

After slipping into a pair of jeans and a T-shirt, I

grabbed my sneakers and headed down the hall. I stepped into my shoes and tied the laces, then moved outside, amazed that night could be so warm. I joined Devon on the sidewalk, and he immediately started walking. He didn't have to ask me whether or not I was going with him. I'd already proven I'd follow him. Glancing at him out of the corner of my eye, I said, "So where are we going exactly?"

"The Playground, of course."

"Why now?"

He kept moving forward, his steps confident, even cocky. "Because night's better."

I didn't ask what night was better for, mostly because I already knew. Everything.

"No, I mean . . . we haven't hung out all week. I haven't even seen you. Why now?"

Devon's smirk spread across his mouth into a smile. "We have revelry to attend to."

"Revelry?" I raised an eyebrow, wondering on what planet a teenage guy said things like that. "And just how often do you guys attend to revelry in the Playground?"

"Every night." He glanced over at me, the low light of the street lamps reflecting briefly in his eyes. "But I thought tonight you might wanna join us."

"Why?" Not that I was complaining. Just curious. And okay, maybe a little insecure after last time.

Devon's shoulders tensed with what seemed like annoyance at all my questions. "Because the boys were asking about you. Because you looked pretty pathetic out there painting that shed today. Because I think you could use some revelry."

Not long after, I was sitting around a bonfire at the back of the Playground with him and his friends. Who needed sleep? I was making memories.

The nameless guys from the other night turned out to have names after all. "Scot, Nick, Cameron—we call him Cam—Thorne, and Markus. Everyone, this is Stephen."

As he spoke their names, I exchanged nods with each of them, making an effort to remember who was who. I remembered Markus from his lock-picking skills, but the others had pretty much been shadows in the dark—something I hoped would change tonight. Already, this time the guys were looking me in the eye and acknowledging my existence, which was a major step in the right direction.

A big paper grocery sack was sitting on the ground by Markus's feet. He reached inside and retrieved a brown bottle with a drawing of a peach on the label. The top of the label read *Dekuyper*. At the bottom were words that sent a nervous tingle through my core: *Original Peachtree Schnapps*. Nervous only because I'd promised my mom a few years ago that I'd stay away from anything heavier than beer until it was legal. She hadn't asked much of me in the way of discipline during our seventeen years together, apart from yelling at me not to drink bleach when I was five and uttering this little gem on my fifteenth birthday: *"No smoking, Stephen. No drugs. And if you insist on sneaking booze, stay away from the hard stuff."*

Because she'd asked so little of me, I felt obligated to listen to all of it. Only . . . now I was in a cemetery, in a crappy town that was looking less and less like a temporary home, surrounded by potential new friends. And my mom was a million miles away. Not just in Denver, but on Mars. Did I still owe her anything? I wasn't sure. All I knew was that when I was seven, she'd uttered another phrase that had stuck with me ever since: *"Make a promise, keep a promise."*

Markus handed the bottle off to the tall guy with the big, broad grin and the dark brown hair—Scot, I thought—who twisted off the cap and took a swig before holding the bottle out to me. I looked at it, not sure what to say or do. I wasn't a partier, but I wasn't straightedge either. There I went again, knowing full well what I wasn't, but not at all what I was.

Meanwhile, Markus passed out more bottles, and I watched as caps were removed and drinks were taken. No one seemed to notice that I hadn't yet taken the bottle from Scot's hand. They were all distracted by their own drinking and by the bonfire they were building. A stack of stray twigs and dead branches had been piled atop one grave, and Devon was using his lighter to start the blaze. Scot shook the bottle at me and smiled, his voice kind of quiet. "It's okay. It tastes sweet."

Reaching out, I took the bottle and brought it closer to my face. As I sniffed the contents, Scot chuckled. "Never drank before, eh?"

Smoke had enveloped the wood pile, and within moments, flames took its place. I wondered what would happen to us if we got caught lighting a fire in a graveyard, let alone drinking. "Just beer. But not much of it. You guys do this a lot?"

"Some." He shrugged and then shook his head. "You don't have to."

Oh, sure. I didn't *have* to drink liquor in the cemetery. Just like I didn't *have* to break into the movie theater. Just like I didn't *have* to go with Devon in the first place. There was always option B: puss out and go home. Of *course* I had to. Who did Scot think he was kidding?

"Where's the Peachtree?" The one Devon had referred to as Cam hurried over. He was short, skinny, and pale, with dirty blond hair and the craziest blue eyes I'd ever seen. Something about those eyes told me that he was an excellent listener. He looked curious and kind. I liked him instantly. Nodding to the bottle in my hand, he reached for it, eyebrows raised. "Hey, you mind?"

Not only didn't I mind, I sighed in relief inside my head where no one else could hear.

Cam took a healthy swig, then placed the bottle right back in my hand.

Damn.

He looked at Scot, and for a moment, I felt invisible. His voice grew softer, and a light entered his eyes that hadn't been there when he was addressing me. "Can we talk later?"

"Yeah." Scot smiled down at Cam, and not only did I *feel* invisible, I was starting to think that I had actually *turned* invisible. No one was in this conversation but Scot and Cam. It made me wonder if they were maybe a couple or something, and I made a mental note to ask one of the other guys later. "Of course."

"Cool." Cam grinned. Before turning to walk away, he gave my shoulder a friendly slap. "Nice to meet ya, man. Stephen, right?"

"Yeah." I nodded. After a moment of just standing there, I looked at the label on the bottle I was holding, as if I were deeply concerned about its ingredients. To my great and apparent interest, it only had seven grams of carbs and seventy-two calories. Fascinating.

Devon appeared beside me, his lips a thin line. "Are you gonna drink it or just stand there pretending to?"

"Make a promise, keep a promise."

But hadn't Mom promised me that she'd always be there for me? Hadn't she and Dad both promised me that we'd always be a family, and that we'd stay in Denver for the rest of our lives? Promises, it seemed, were made to be broken.

Deciding I'd kept my promise long enough, I lifted the bottle to my lips, and time slowed a bit as I felt this weird sense of losing something I couldn't get back. That is, right up until the moment the liquid poured into my mouth and I swallowed. Then my throat momentarily caught fire and smoke rolled out of my mouth and ears. It was pretty much like a Bugs Bunny cartoon. And if you have a problem with me equating my first real drinking experience with a beloved childhood cartoon . . . you have deeper issues than me.

I looked at the label again, this time in disgust. If that crap contained acid, you'd think the manufacturer would have said something. "Peach, my ass. It tastes like syrup."

"In six more swallows, you won't give a shit."

"I could use some of that," I said. "Not giving a shit."

"Then get to it, man. But don't hog the schnapps. There's plenty more else to drink." Devon snatched the bottle out of my hand, his absolute annoyance coming through loud and clear. I couldn't tell if he was irritated with me and my indecision or if he was just having a mood swing. Either way, I knew it was probably best that I kept any questions to myself.

Scot must have felt the same way. "Hey, Cam. You wanna talk now?"

Cam and the big guy, Thorne, were thumb wrestling, but it took only a word from Scot to pull Cam away. "I thought you wanted to wait."

Scot shrugged. "I'm done waiting."

Scot followed Cam away from the fire, and I stood there awkwardly for a moment, not really sure how I was supposed to react. I guess it showed, because right then Markus came over to me and pulled a short, rectangular bottle from the bag. The liquid inside was bright green, almost fluorescent. It didn't look like something any human should ingest. On the front, it said *MD 20/20*, which made it sound more like a chemical than a drink. He tilted his head curiously at me. "Mad Dog? They say it's kiwi-and-lemon flavored, but if you ask me, it tastes like I imagine antifreeze would."

"I'll pass," I said, wrinkling my nose. Scot and Cam were disappearing into the woods on the edge of the cemetery. If I was wrong about my impression of them, I was seriously curious about where they were going. I glanced at Markus, not wanting to ask because it was really none of my business, but wanting to know just the same. If it weren't for my curiosity, I'd never know anything. "So . . . about Scot and Cam. Are those two—"

"A thing? Yeah. But they still haven't admitted it to

anyone. Not even us." He looked at me then, suddenly guarded. "You don't have a problem with that, do ya?"

"Of course not." I'd had gay friends in the past—knew lots of gay people back in Colorado. It didn't matter to me what someone's orientation was. I guess it just surprised me to find this kind of tolerance in such a small, otherwise backward place. Open minds were everywhere, it seemed. How closed-minded of me to presume otherwise.

Finally accepting my reluctance to drink something that tasted like automobile lubricant, Markus dropped the Mad Dog back in the bag. "Good. Because I know for a fact that every guy here would kick your ass for giving them a hard time. Scot and Cam are cool. And we protect our own."

Shrugging, I said, "I was just curious."

Markus raised his left eyebrow at me. "*Curious* curious? Or just curious?"

It took me a moment to realize what he was asking, but when it occurred to me, I shook my head. "What? No. I'm straight."

He nodded like that was pretty much what he'd expected. Then, he snapped his fingers and dug around in the bottom of the paper sack. It was a huge bag, with endless possibilities. I kept waiting for him to pull out a lamp or an umbrella or something, but instead he retrieved a bottle of what looked like pink wine. The label read *Boone's Farm Strawberry*

Hill. Placing the bottle in my hand, Markus smiled brightly. "You, my new friend, need some time on the farm."

I twisted the cap off and sniffed. What was inside smelled sweet and appealing, so I took a sip, and then took a bigger swallow. Finally, something that didn't set my head on fire or make me gag at the thought of drinking it. Markus, who was apparently the group's personal bartender, looked pleased.

"Stephen, right?" As I was helping myself to another swallow, I turned my head to see Thorne, staggering a bit to the right, like we were on a cruise ship or something. My guess was that Thorne had likely spent a bit of time on the farm already tonight. He grabbed my shoulder with one meaty hand to steady himself and then breathed hotly into my face. "Hey, Stephen. How can you tell which squirrel is in charge?"

I sincerely hoped he was telling a joke and not asking me a question that he needed a serious answer to. Drunk people could be pretty obnoxious. "I . . . don't know. How?"

"He's the one with the biggest nuts." Thorne bent over with laughter. He was the only one. Markus and I just stood there, waiting. I took another drink, and Markus borrowed the bottle long enough to take one of his own.

When Thorne straightened and looked at me, I shrugged, not wanting to offend him. Even though it had been one of the worst jokes that I had ever heard, I said, "Oh. Funny."

The fire was burning brightly by this point, hot coals glowing at its core. At the edges of the cemetery, fireflies glowed intermittently. The stars shone above us. So much light, and yet the darkness seemed so much bigger, so much more.

"All right, then. What do you call a cheap circumcision?" Thorne took the wine bottle from my hand and downed a generous mouthful before handing it to me. He wiped the excess from his mouth with the back of his hand and said, "A rip-off."

I cringed, swallowing a bit more of that Strawberry Hill. My entire body was warm, and I was feeling pretty mellow. A cursory glance informed me that I'd already drunk half the bottle, with only a little help from Markus and Thorne. I must have been buzzed, because I actually laughed at Thorne's stupid joke. Markus, who was clearly more sober than I was, winced and said, "Your jokes are really stupid, Thorne."

"Yeah," I said. "If you could just try maybe . . . *not* telling any more, that'd be . . . great." The three of us stood there for a moment in silence. Then Markus lost it, laughing, and I joined him. Thorne blinked a lot. My guess was that he was pretty wasted.

"Wanna hear a joke about a broken pencil? Never mind,

it's pointless!" Thorne laughed loudly and wandered back to Nick, the only guy I hadn't talked to yet. They slapped hands in a high five, but Nick looked reluctant to do so. Something told me I'd like Thorne a whole lot better when he was sober.

I took another swig. "So. Anyway."

"Yeah. We can just pretend that whole thing never happened," Markus said. "Have you met Nick yet?"

As I shook my head, I felt a wave of pleasant dizziness overtake me. Yup. Definitely buzzed. "Not yet."

"He and Thorne are brothers. Nick's the quieter one. You'd like him." I wouldn't have guessed that Nick and Thorne were related if Markus hadn't said so. But once he did, I could see the resemblance. Same green eyes, same broad shoulders. Nick was certainly far leaner than his hulking brother. Still, they looked more alike than Devon and Cara, who were twins.

Devon was perched on top of the tallest tombstone in the cemetery, a nearly empty bottle of whiskey in one hand and a clove cigarette in the other. At the base of the tombstone lay the empty bottle of schnapps, but Devon appeared completely sober and unamused. Not unhappy. Just . . . unamused. I looked up at him, towering over all of us, and bet that if we were squirrels, Devon would be the one in charge. Snorting with laughter, I spit out a mouthful of cheap wine and nearly shot it from my nose.

So this was what it felt like to be drunk. Or getting drunk. Or something.

Noticing that I'd finished the last of the Boone's Farm, Devon dropped his whiskey bottle down to Markus and gestured to me with a nod. Markus handed the bottle to me, and I took it in my hand, marveling at the amber liquid as it licked at the glass like fire. Devon's eyes were on me, locked in sudden intrigue at what I would do next. Cheap strawberry wine and sugary peach booze were the stuff of teenagers, the stuff of kids playing around with drinking, the stuff of children pretending to be adults. Whiskey . . . that was what men drank. Was I a boy, or was I a man?

With a nod at Devon, I pressed the bottle to my lips, tilting it up. As I swallowed, I resisted the urge to cough and swear and puke my guts out. Whiskey, it turned out, was nasty shit. I wasn't at all sure how Devon could stomach the stuff. I looked at the bottle in my hand, and wondered if what was contained inside could really define whether someone was a boy or a man. I doubted it.

I was still doubting it when Devon tossed me a tiny, airplane-serving-sized bottle of vodka. He took a drag on his cigarette and held up a tiny bottle of his own. Then he nodded, the hint of something sinister glinting in his eyes. "You and me, Stephen. First one to finish wins."

"Wins what?" I was tempted to say, *Your sister?* but didn't, attributing my snarky bravery to the bottle in my hand. Liquid bravery or not, I wasn't sure if Devon was in a joking mood, and figured that a little quip like that might earn me a punch in the face. I hadn't told Devon about making out with Cara in the rain, and I wouldn't, either. I was smarter than that, at least.

Devon looked at me pointedly. "Just drink."

Slowly, and with no way out—not without losing some serious cool points, anyway—I twisted the tiny cap off and met Devon's gaze with a daring, raised eyebrow. Devon tossed his cap over his shoulder. It bounced, then rolled for several feet until it finally disappeared over the edge of the cliff that led to the reservoir below.

In my head, I heard the theme from *The Good, the Bad and the Ugly*—the one they always play when the sheriff and the bad guy face off—and suppressed a chuckle. Then I tilted the bottle up, drinking for real this time. The vodka burned, too, but not as much as the whiskey had. It also tasted like shit.

Just as I swallowed the last drop, Devon's empty bottle hit me in the knee. I shook my head, defeated. "Guess that means you win."

Devon's eyes lit up. The corners of his mouth curled into a smile. Devon always won. That much was written all over his face. The flickering light of the fire made him look even more sinister. "Yes, it does. Wanna see what?"

I shrugged, my stomach gurgling in protest. "Sure."

Devon licked his lips, appearing to taste the remaining liquor on them, and turned to Markus. "Hey, Markus . . . if all your friends jumped off a cliff, would you?"

Markus grinned. "You're damn right I would."

Devon seemed to be mulling something over in his mind. After a moment, he turned his attention back to Markus. The air felt heavier. Just before Devon spoke, I realized that all the boys in the group were watching me, as if waiting for my reaction to whatever was coming. In clear, crisp words that seemed to echo into the air, Devon said, "But would you jump first?"

Markus squeezed his hands into fists, cracking the knuckles. Then he broke into a run. His feet slapped the ground in beat with my heart as he came ever closer to the cliff's edge. I flicked my eyes from Markus to Devon, who stood tall and proud, looking down on the scene from well above the rest of us. He seemed to be watching me far more than he was watching Markus.

I turned back to Markus, who ran until there was no more room on that dirt road left to run. He dove off the edge with his arms stretched out in front of him and his toes pointed, a form that would have made Superman proud. As his feet left the ground, I bolted for the edge of the cliff and skidded to a halt, wavering as my feet hit the loose soil. My booze-soaked world shifted wildly, but I managed to catch myself before I followed Markus's lead over the edge. Several rocks weren't so lucky and tumbled over after him. I looked down, searching the reservoir frantically, but there was nothing below besides rock and water. Markus was nowhere to be found. He'd simply vanished. There'd been no splash, no ripples in the water. He'd dived into the reservoir, but I hadn't heard him break the surface.

The crunch of gravel sounded as Devon dropped down from the tombstone and came to stand beside me. Leaning slightly over the edge, I was still searching the water for Markus's body. I must have missed the sound of him hitting the water because I'd been drinking. My perception had been drowned to nothing by whiskey, vodka, and schnapps. A theory formulated in my drunken brain that I couldn't see him because he'd hit hard enough to sink, and then was carried off downstream. That, or he'd climbed inside an old refrigerator. My heart raged in my chest.

Markus was dead.

I stared in horror at Devon, who merely nodded casually, as if this was to be expected. Devon took a long, slow drag on his clove cigarette, and flicked the butt over the edge of the cliff. All I could do was stare after it, saying nothing, watching the ember do somersaults through the air. After an eternity, it was swallowed by the reservoir.

Dead. Markus was dead.

I couldn't wrap my head around it. We had to get to the police. Now. Maybe there was still time to save him. I took a step back—my disbelieving eyes locked on the ledge, my heart pounding out an urgent rhythm—and I turned to run. But a soft body blocked my way. I slammed into it and hit the ground with a thump. My fingers were shaking as I brushed the gravel from them and looked up at whoever I'd run into.

Markus grinned down at me, and Nick and Thorne burst into laughter behind him. Markus nodded once at Devon, who returned the favor.

I stared at Markus. I looked back to the ledge. When I confirmed one more time that Markus was indeed standing right there in front of me, my heart calmed a little, but I remained confused. My head was swimming, and the liquor didn't help. "How did . . . but you . . ."

Nick tossed a bottle to Markus and he caught it, then took a swig, as if replenishing himself. As he wiped his mouth dry with the back of his hand, he said, "You wanna know how I did it?"

I swallowed hard, a bitter taste coating my tongue. "Of course I do."

Devon plucked a Zippo lighter from his pocket and I noticed the small skull on the front of it as he lit another cigarette. His jaw tensed as he drew the smoke into his lungs, his voice gravelly. "Are you sure, Stephen? Because once you know it, you can't unknow it."

Running over the details in my mind of what had just happened—Markus running, jumping, falling, then appearing once again unharmed—I nodded, still terribly confused. I had to know.

Nick spoke up. "Show him, already. Show him so we can stop pretending."

Devon's eyes flicked to the cliff's edge. "I don't know if you can handle it, Stephen. It's a long way down."

Brushing the remaining gravel from my hands, I stood and looked over the ledge again. I wasn't sure what the distance had to do with the trick he'd just pulled, or whether they were just trying to psych me out again. I was about to call Devon's bluff when he slammed into me, clutching me close in a pseudowrestling move. I lost my footing and we tumbled over the edge together.

Wind whipped by me, pulling my hair from my face, ruffling my clothes as we fell. Terrified, I clutched Devon. He was clutching me, too, but his grip seemed far less panicked, far less certain that we were going to die. My thoughts were a scramble of terror. DeadI'mdeadI'mdeadI'mdeadI'm dead!

"Stephen!" Devon's voice sounded very far away, even

though his face was right there by my left ear. "Get ready!"

The rocks below grew larger and larger. The water reached up for us, hungry. It was going to swallow us whole.

DeadI'mdeadI'mdeadI'mdeadI'mdead!

"Look at me, Stephen!"

I couldn't. I couldn't take my eyes off the rocks, the water, our impending demise.

DeadI'mdeadI'mdeadI'mdeadI'mdead!!!

"Now!"

With enormous effort, I met Devon's eyes. They were the last thing that I would ever see. He was the last person I would ever look at. Because I was going to die. Devon was my murderer. Devon was my friend. And it was all over. I screamed.

And screamed.

And screamed.

Devon landed on the balls of his feet and stumbled back, catching me as we hit a ledge that I couldn't see from where we had been standing overhead. He pulled me back from the edge and I whipped my head around, wondering how I could have missed the outcropping of land that we were now standing on, how I hadn't been able to see it from up top. My screams died down pitifully as the realization hit me that I was safe. I was alive. My right ankle was throbbing from the awkward way I'd hit the ground, but I was alive.

Still catching his breath, Devon pointed to the trail that led up the side of the cliff back to the cemetery. "You should've seen your face. Classic."

I shoved Devon hard with both hands. He wavered, but didn't fall. His jaw clenched when my hands made contact, as if I were *this close* to pissing him off. I didn't care. "What the hell, Devon! What the hell was that?"

As I stormed up the cliff's trail, Devon called after me through the chorus of laughter. Laughter from his friends— not my friends, not our friends, *his* friends. "It was just a joke, Stephen. Lighten up."

I didn't want to lighten up. I didn't want to be the butt of his joke. I just wanted to forget this night had ever happened.

But on my walk home, all I could picture were Devon's eyes, and how it had felt to know he'd be the last person I'd ever see. I wasn't going to forget that any time soon.

chapter 7

The next morning I was up by dawn, but I didn't move more than an inch or so from my bed. My mind was still spinning with thoughts that I couldn't wrap my brain around, swirling like the water of the reservoir had the night before. The image played over and over again inside my mind, as if the backs of my eyelids were a movie screen and I was the unwilling audience to a film I'd rather forget. We'd been standing in the cemetery, joking around, and then suddenly I'd thought I was dying. I'd known I was dying. And it was all just a big joke.

Not to mention the fact that I was pretty sure I was

actually dying now . . . owing to all the booze I'd drunk.

This might have been a hangover, but I really had no frame of reference. My head felt like a big, pain-filled balloon, and the room was kind of tilting on its own. Apparently, I couldn't hold my liquor. I was okay with that. I didn't want to hold liquor—mine or anybody else's. I didn't ever want to see alcohol again. I just wanted to puke my guts out and fall asleep for several millennia. But that wasn't going to happen. Because I didn't live with people who believed in peace and quiet. I lived with—

"Where is that boy?"

—my grandmother and—

"Stephen! For crying out loud, it's noon. Get up!"

—my dad, who either didn't give a crap that I was hungover, or else had no clue. I was hoping for that last one.

I rolled carefully out of bed to a semi-standing, semi-hunched-over position, bracing myself on the footboard, then the doorjamb as I made my way out of my room and down the hall to the kitchen. The moment the light from the front bay window hit my eyes, a sharp pain slashed through my head. I didn't just feel like I was going to die. I kind of wanted to. But first, I wanted to puke and get it over with.

My dad was sitting in a kitchen chair, and the moment he looked at me, as I fell into the chair beside him, I could tell he knew that I'd been out drinking the night before. I tried to sit up straight and pretend that I was fine, but when I did, something sick coated the back of my throat. So I slumped down in my seat and laid my head on the table. You know. Praying for death and all that.

"Stephen, maybe you should go take a shower before joining your grandmother and me for lunch."

I muttered something unintelligible in response.

"Stephen." His tone was calm, but I could tell that he was in the mood to shout. So I dragged myself out of the chair and down the hall to the bathroom, swaying this way and that as the room tilted even more dramatically.

To my credit, I didn't get sick. Despite the fact that the toilet was right there and on my side completely. *It's okay, buddy*, the toilet said. *I've got your back. Toss those cookies in here and get on with your day.*

I have no idea why the toilet called me buddy. Give me a break, I was hungover.

The shower was hot and calmed my headache a bit, and after I got out, I felt a bit less like the world was tilting on its side. I also didn't feel the least bit hungry. But I'd heard my dad's tone, and I figured I had better join them at the table, or else there would be hell to pay. Not that I wasn't paying it already.

When I returned to the kitchen, there were three plates on the table. My grandmother was at the stove, but she kept glancing at the kitchen window into the backyard. Likely she was making plans for whatever household improvement Dad and I could do next.

I took my seat again and tried not to make eye contact. Dad nudged a glass of water toward me and quietly said, "Sip it slowly, but drink it all. And take these."

Then he handed me two Tylenol. Which was the precise moment I realized that my dad was being pretty cool about this whole thing. The shower, the water, the pain meds. He was trying to help me rather than punish me. I wasn't sure why. He should have been pissed. Mom would have been pissed.

I took the pills in my hand and said, "Thanks."

I didn't eat much lunch, but I put a lot of effort into moving food around my plate in a creative manner. Once my dad had cleared the plates away, he nodded toward my bedroom, as if to excuse me. Gratefully, I made my way back down the hall and collapsed into bed.

When I woke again, it was dark. I had managed to sleep the entire day. I didn't feel quite so much like death, at least, but the movie playing in my mind about Devon, the cliff, and my imminent doom still refused to stop playing. I had to know what exactly had happened the night before. I had to know if it really had been a joke, and it only seemed so terrifying because I was tipsy, or if Devon really had been trying to kill us both and just messed up. I didn't even want to consider the third option—that I was losing my mind. I mean, the idea of going crazy scared the shit out of me, what with my mom and all.

After throwing on my shoes, I made my way quietly out the front door and across town to the Playground. I wasn't surprised to see the boys there this time, or the bonfire they'd built on one of the graves. To them, it seemed, this was pleasure as usual.

The flames cast eerie shadows of the boys onto the tombstones and the trees—elongated forms that made them look alien, strange. I kept my attention on Devon, who was standing apart from the group, looking up into the night sky with a dreamlike expression on his face. He was dressed in shades of black and gray, and I suspected that the grays had all been blacks at one time. I gave his shoulder a shove—light enough not to start anything, but firm enough to show him I meant business. "What the hell was that, Devon?"

He barely flinched, but I could tell by the set of his mouth that he wanted to react. I wondered what made him stop, but then recognized his inaction for what it was: patience. I was still learning my place in their little group, and Devon was being forgiving of my actions. For now.

From his shirt pocket, he withdrew a semicrushed packet of clove cigarettes. He held it out to me, but I shook my head. Drinking was one thing. Smoking was absolutely another, and I refused to cross that line. When he could tell I wasn't going to change my mind, he popped one into his mouth with a shrug, lit it with his skull lighter, and returned both to his pocket. It took him two inhales and exhales to formulate a response to my question. He didn't meet my eyes, but as he exhaled, he said, "What the hell was what?"

Behind us, Scot, Cam, and Thorne broke into laughter over something I hadn't heard or seen. Shortly after, I heard music playing, which meant that one of them had likely brought out a radio or iPod or something. The song was one I'd listened to myself a hundred times, the singer rambling on and on about knowing what I did in the dark.

What was I so worried about? Maybe it was just a stupid joke gone wrong. Maybe it was nothing to get pissed about in the grand scheme of things. But still. "Last night. The cliff. You know what I mean."

"You were pretty drunk, my friend." He sucked on his cigarette, making the ember glow brightly. As he blew out a ring of smoke, the light from the ember dimmed. His face looked gaunt in the semidarkness. "Maybe you fell. Maybe I saved your ass and you totally overreacted."

I tried to fix the night before in my mind—recall every moment leading up to falling over the edge—but couldn't. Most of it was a blur. But Devon's eyes . . . and that sensation of knowing I was about to die . . . that much I could recall. "I didn't fall on my own."

"It was just a joke. Call it an initiation, if you will. And for what it's worth, I'm sorry. It's not often we accept anyone into our little group. We like you, Stephen. The boys like you. I like you. It just went too far." He met my gaze then and held it for a good, long time. This wasn't the face of a guy who was trying to screw with me, or dupe me in any way. This was the face of a guy who'd welcomed me into his group of friends without, I guess, much hazing at all. Just a quick warning about his sister and my balls, and after that, a harmless prank. I'd known a group of guys back in Denver who'd required an act of violence in exchange for acceptance into their little club. That was serious. This was nothing. So why was I being such a jerk to him over some bad joke gone wrong?

Sighing heavily, I ran my right hand through my hair, raking it back from my face. "We could have gotten seriously hurt."

Devon finished his cigarette and then dropped it on the ground. "Don't be such a pussy. Come on."

Once we reached the group, Devon made the kill sign, slashing his finger across his neck. Immediately, Thorne turned off the music and all eyes were on Devon. Devon said, "So, Stephen just asked me what the hell we were doing last night here in the Playground."

To my left, Markus snorted. "If I remember it right, a shitload of vodka."

"But mostly schnapps," Nick chimed in.

Devon let them have their laugh, but then said something that made the very air change. It felt heavier, somehow, and tasted kind of metallic. But maybe that was the last of the hangover talking. Devon said, "He seems pretty worried that we might throw him off a cliff or something."

I glanced at the others, who were all watching him quietly, fearfully, as if waiting for him to speak again. I cleared my throat in embarrassment. Why had I come here tonight? Even if I was remembering right about the cliff and all, why did I feel the need to break up the party? Maybe I was determined to ruin the small bit of happiness I'd found here in Spencer. Maybe I didn't really believe that I deserved happiness anywhere.

Without waiting for their response or approval—he needed neither, when it boiled down to it—Devon looked directly at me. "Like I said last night: once you know it, you can't unknow it. You're either in, or you're out. We want you in. In on all of our secrets. In on all of our fun. But we don't let people in lightly. So be careful with your choice here, Stephen."

Everyone seemed very concerned about my ability to make the right choices lately. Everyone but me. I seemed happy enough to let everyone else make the decisions for me.

Devon stepped up to me. The group hushed, like maybe we were going to brawl or something. I hoped not. Devon was lean, but he looked tough. And I'd never been in a fistfight before. In a low voice, he said, "So. Are you in . . . or not?"

I looked around at the boys and, last, at Devon. "What happens if I'm not?"

Markus and the other boys laughed like I'd just said the funniest thing they'd ever heard. Devon shrugged casually, but something about the light in his eyes said that he was feeling anything but casual at the moment. Maybe I'd surprised him with my response. Or maybe I was wrong and he didn't really give a crap what I wanted. "Only one way to find out."

I glanced at Markus, who offered me a reassuring smile. Then I met Devon's eyes, wondering what exactly I was getting myself into. I swallowed hard. It was my life. And it was my choice how I decided to live it. With a nod, I said, "I'm in."

Devon wore a small, knowing smile, as if he'd never had a doubt. "Then let's do this." Thorne turned up the music again and Markus placed a bottle in my hand. I had no idea what was in it, or even whether I could really trust this group of guys. I just knew that I wanted this moment to last, and I didn't care what came next.

Now mattered. Not *then*. Not *someday*. But *now*.

I pressed the bottle to my lips, tipping it up, letting the clear fluid empty into my mouth, burning my throat. A hand backlit by the bonfire reached out and lifted the bottle farther, and I drank and drank until it was empty. I knew that hand belonged to Devon. I knew that he and the boys probably got piss drunk in the cemetery every night, all summer long. But I didn't care. I just wanted to belong. And forget. And enjoy.

The evening became a happy blur. At one point, Devon challenged me to a race back into town—just him and me. The boys all paused then, watching us with expectant looks on their faces. I wasn't sure how to read them. Did they feel left out? Annoyed? I wasn't sure.

Once Devon said the words, we both stood there, facing each other, waiting to see if the other would go through with it and run. Devon moved first, so fast that I might have fallen behind if I'd hesitated for even a moment more. But I darted after him, my lungs burning, my legs aching as we moved from dirt path to asphalt to sidewalk. We ran until my stomach cramped from laughter, and when we reached William Spencer's mansion, Devon began to climb. I followed, pulling myself up on grates and pipes while planting my feet on bricks that stood out from the building's surface. I used whatever footholds and handholds I could find, and we scaled the building all the way to the roof. Devon was first to reach it, and he balanced his way to the small tower at the very top, gripping the weather vane with his right hand to steady himself. I climbed up beside him, knowing that Devon had won the race, but not giving a damn.

The night sky stretched out above us, an endless velvet blanket riddled with millions of bright holes. I was feeling breathless, but not out of breath. Tired, but not at all ready to sleep. This was our time—the midnight hour—and there wasn't a single damn thing that anyone else could do about it.

From way up here, the town of Spencer looked beautiful. Magical, almost. I took it all in for a moment before speaking. "So, I gotta ask. What would you have done to me if I'd said I wasn't in?"

"Killed you."

He hadn't even hesitated before answering, and there wasn't so much as a hint of a smile in his expression.

"You're full of shit." I was pretty sure he wasn't, but what did I know? Too little, I feared.

"So's the world, Stephen. It's also full of monsters with friendly faces."

I shrugged. "Yeah, well. You're still full of shit."

A smile touched his lips, but faded quickly as he looked out over the town. "From up here, it almost looks like a nice place to live."

A chuckle escaped me. "Alcohol has a way of making things look different."

"Maybe that's not such a bad thing." He withdrew a flask from an inside pocket and unscrewed the cap, offering me a swig. When I shook my head, he took a gulp of whatever was inside, then closed the flask and put it away. "Tell me about Denver."

I shrugged, taken aback some by his sudden interest in my past. "What's to tell? It's cold in the winter, but the people are nice."

"I bet the mountains are awesome." His expression looked almost dreamy, and I wondered for a moment exactly how much booze he could handle before falling off a roof.

"Why just bet on it? Why not move there?"

Storms rolled into his eyes, casting out the dreams that had been there. "You don't get it, Stephen. Some towns are like glue. And some people are just stuck. Entire families, man. For generations."

"What about after high school? Why not apply to college somewhere else? Or get a job and move?"

Venom invaded him then, as if my suggestion really angered him. "Because some people don't have the luxury of choice, Stephen. And I'm one of them. I have a D average at an already crappy school. I'm stuck. In goddamn Spencer, Michigan. Until the day I die."

We both went quiet for a few minutes, until finally, Devon broke our collective silence. "Cara was asking about you."

A record needle immediately scratched across the soundtrack that had been playing inside my mind. I swallowed hard, trying to keep my obvious interest in the subject hidden behind a curtain of aloofness. "Yeah?"

Devon took a deep breath and blew it out through his nose, not meeting my eyes. "Yeah."

Without saying anything else, he climbed down from the tower, onto the main roof. As I began to follow, he gestured to my feet and to the loose shingles. But when he spoke, I knew that he wasn't concerned for my safety. He was talking about Cara, and reminding me of our little conversation by the reservoir the night we met.

He said, "Watch your step."

Despite the fact that it was in the eighties and sticky-hot, I felt a chill in the air. One that could only be attributed to the strange undercurrent of fear that I had of Devon, and the understanding that no one, apparently, was allowed anywhere near his sister without his consent. But I couldn't leave Cara alone now. It was too late for that. It was too late for a lot of things.

chapter 8

Dropping down the last few feet to the grass below, I looked up at the mansion, amazed that we'd climbed so high—especially without getting caught or breaking our necks. Devon was already on the ground waiting for me, as if to make sure that I made it down okay. After I landed, we made our way to the sidewalk, where Devon lit another clove cigarette. The smoke smelled sweet, like pipe tobacco. But that didn't mean I enjoyed it being blown in my face.

Devon's attention was focused on a car making its way slowly down the street toward us. It was small and sporty, and in the soft light of the streetlamps, it looked to be a cool, metallic blue. Nothing at all like Dad's crappy Beetle.

Devon inhaled sharply, making the ember on his cigarette glow orange, as the car came to a stop beside where we were standing. The driver's-side window buzzed as it went down. Lane leaned out and gestured for me to come closer. Lane's friend Casey was sitting in the passenger seat. After a moment's hesitation, I approached the car. "Hey, Lane. What's up?"

"Need a ride?" The inside of the car reeked of cheap beer. So much for his ice-cream-social image.

"Nah. I can walk. It's not far."

"Sure you'd rather walk? Might not be safe." His eyes moved immediately behind me to Devon—an action that was both arrogant and insulting. He was implying that Devon was some kind of criminal . . . and while, okay, that might not be far from the truth, he had no business pointing it out to me or anyone else. Lane didn't bother lowering his voice when he spoke again. He might've spoken a little louder, just to be sure that Devon heard him. "You know that guy?"

I looked over my shoulder at Devon, who took another drag on his smoke before dropping it to the ground and grinding it into dust with his shoe. I couldn't read what he was thinking for sure in his expression, but I thought I had a pretty good guess. I turned back to Lane, making sure to keep my voice just as loud as his so that Devon would definitely hear. "Yeah. We're friends."

Lane pursed his lips, looking very much like he was holding back a mouthful of vomit. What was it about a guy like Devon that made a guy like Lane sick? Or was he about to retch over having misjudged me for a fellow racquetball fiend? His top lip twitched as he said, "You should be more careful who you make friends with, Stephen. That whole family is trash."

Backing up, I returned to my place on the sidewalk beside Devon. "I am careful. Thanks."

Lane hit the gas and his tires spun until they squealed, sending smoke and the smell of burnt rubber into the air. As Lane peeled away, Devon flipped him the bird.

I shook my head. "That guy is such a douche."

Devon shrugged, his eyes still keenly locked on Lane's retreating vehicle. "He doesn't matter."

"And he knows it," I said. "A guy like Lane? He'll never matter." The smoke from Lane's tires settled onto the pavement before disappearing.

"Will any of us?" Devon cocked an eyebrow at me, and I found myself speechless for a moment. It had sounded like an admission of self-doubt, but that couldn't be. A guy like Devon was in charge, confident, and never doubted anything. Did he?

In the grass behind us, a cricket chirped its opinion. My

mouth felt dry, in spite of or maybe because of all the drinking I'd done. "You headin' home?" I said.

"Not yet." He turned on his heel and headed back down the sidewalk, in the direction of the Playground. Offering me a halfhearted salute over his shoulder, he said, "Later."

"Later." The word fell flat in the surrounding night air.

The walk home was quiet and empty—the way that small towns get once the sun goes down. In the distance, I could hear a dog yowling, but even that didn't last. No one was outside, and the air had that heavy feeling of after midnight. I wasn't scared or uneasy. Just peaceful. Maybe this place wasn't so bad after all.

Stopping at a light on the end of my street, I looked up hopefully at Cara's house, and it must have been my lucky night, because there was Cara sitting on her front porch swing. Her eyes were downcast, her hands folded delicately in her lap. As I moved closer, I saw the glint of tears on her cheeks, which made my feet move faster. When I stepped up on the porch, the boards beneath my feet creaked, drawing her attention. She dried her eyes with the palms of her hands and I sat next to her, not saying anything at all, not knowing what a guy was supposed to say when he found a girl he cared for crying her eyes out in the middle of the night. We sat there together, swinging slowly. After a while, I reached out and took her hand in mine. Then I waited. For what, I didn't know. For whatever Cara needed me to wait for, I guessed.

Fireflies lit up the front yard—bright spots amid the darkness. I watched them, occasionally squeezing Cara's hand, reminding her that I was next to her. With her.

Finally, she spoke, her voice raspy, as if her tears had been pouring for a long time before I'd found her there. "She's crazy, y'know. Everyone sees it. Everyone knows it. But no one talks about it. My mom is crazy, my dad is gone, Devon might as well be gone. Meanwhile, the only money we've got comes from life insurance checks, and I'm left here, picking up the pieces of her crazy every day."

I didn't want to lie to her. I didn't want to tell her what everyone had probably already told her before. That her mom just needed some time, that her dad was in a better place now, that Devon would come back to her eventually. I wanted to tell her the truth. "Your brother's a jerk for leaving this all on you. It sucks that you lost your dad. And you're right. Martha is crazy."

For a moment, I wondered if I was doing the right thing—maybe she really had wanted me to spout some bullshit about how everything was going to be okay. But then I looked into her eyes and saw relief. Relief that someone had recognized what a truly shitty situation she was stuck in. Relief that someone understood.

She squeezed my hand and said, "She didn't used to be. But seeing my dad die just totally broke her. She has been a raving lunatic ever since."

I hated to ask, but had to. "What happened to him?"

"He was chief of police of this shit-hole town, y'know. But it was better back then. My mom was totally normal. A little distant, but normal—reachable, y'know?"

I didn't, but I nodded anyway. I was surprised to hear her dad had been the chief of police, considering how Devon and Cara both seemed to live just outside the law. But maybe that was the point. And Cara needed someone to understand. She needed someone to listen, and I wanted to hear every word she had to say.

"I used to catch him and my mom slow dancing in the kitchen to an old song by the Smiths called 'Please, Please, Please Let Me Get What I Want.' It was sweet." A brief smile brushed her lips, but quickly faded away. As if in response, the fireflies lighting up her front yard dimmed.

"Then one night he went investigating something at the Playground. Everything changed after that. The official report says some homeless guy killed him and then got away. Of course"—she sighed the words more than spoke them— "that's not what my mom says."

"What's Martha's theory?" Cara's hand fit perfectly in mine. I couldn't help but notice how soft her fingers were. Almost fragile.

After a moment of silence, I realized that she was looking at me, her perfect bottom lip pinched between her teeth. She looked worried. Or frightened. Maybe both. I was about to ask why when she said, "She thinks the Winged Ones got him."

My heart beat twice before I could speak again. "Oh."

"Yeah." Slowly, she slipped her hand away from mine and placed it in her lap.

I didn't know what to say. "This town really loves its legends, eh?"

"You could say that." A light breeze passed, brushing her hair into her eyes for a moment and then brushing it back. She didn't speak again, which meant that I kind of had to. The only real problem was that I had no idea what to say.

"So . . . basically . . . Martha saw him killed, lost her mind, and now blames his death on some monsters with wings that bring tragedy down on one single small Michigan town's population?"

"Pretty much." Cara shifted in her seat, as if she was suddenly growing uncomfortable. I wondered if I'd said or done something wrong.

"Hey," I said, reaching out and brushing her arm with

my knuckles. "Are you mad at me?"

"No. I just . . ." She released a sigh. "You're making fun of me."

Shaking my head, I captured her hand once again. This time, she didn't immediately lace her fingers with mine. "I am not. I'm just agreeing with you that your mom might be one French fry short of a Happy Meal."

"I know. It's just . . . she's still my mom. Y'know?" She shrugged with one shoulder, and I got it. Martha, for all her crazy faults, was still the woman who'd given birth to Cara, who'd given her Devon, who probably had wiped away her tears as a kid. And no one outside of that relationship had any right to speak ill of her.

"I get it." She frowned doubtfully, so I took a deep breath and readied the heavy words on my tongue. "My mom lives in an asylum."

Her eyes popped open wider then, and I gave it a second to sink in that I wasn't lying or trying to top her issues with her own mom. I just wanted her to see that if anyone outside of her immediate family understood her situation, it was me. But if I was going to be honest with her, I needed to be honest with myself—something I struggled with on a daily basis. "One day she started ranting about her own brand of monsters, actually, and she just never stopped. They thought she was schizophrenic, then they thought maybe she was suffering from dementia, but now the doctors aren't sure what it is. Whatever she has, it seems to be permanent. All they can do is keep her doped up and locked away, so that she's not 'a danger to herself or others.' My dad is looking for a new job, but he has to find a place with a good facility nearby so we can move Mom near us, too. Until then, we're pretty much stuck, and so is she."

Cara's eyes shimmered in the low light. In the yard, the fireflies began to glow again, a small glimmer of hope amid the darkness. She gave my hand a squeeze. Gentle. Caring. Understanding. "I'm sorry about your mom."

"I'm sorry about your mom, too." I swallowed, forcing tears back down my throat. I cried hard the day my mom was admitted, and promised myself that that would be the last time I shed tears over something I couldn't control. "I miss her. And it kills me to say it, but I kinda blame her for my life sucking—apart from this, I mean." I gave her hand a squeeze. As if to let me know how much she understood, she squeezed back. It meant more to me than she could possibly know. "Without the hospital bills, we would have been okay. But . . . I guess it doesn't matter. I just keep wishing the phone would ring and we'd get news that she's all better now and coming home. How stupid is that? To wish for something that will never happen? But still . . . I miss her."

Cara nodded, getting it completely. Getting me—like no one ever had before. "I miss my mom, too. It wouldn't be so bad if Devon would just help out more, y'know? But he's totally avoided us since Dad died. Now all he does is drink at the Playground."

"It's probably his way of dealing with it. Some people just can't handle death." I glanced at her then, and kept my voice hushed out of respect. "He told me about his friend drowning. Bobby."

"That kid was a putz. If you ask me, Devon's better off without him." Her words were so sudden, so cold in the midnight air, I half expected to see them leave her lips in a puff of fog. But then she looked at me, and all that had troubled me about what she'd just said disappeared in an instant. She was dressed in mourner's black, and despite her tears, her thick, dark eyeliner remained. Her eyes shimmered in the aftermath of her sadness. My gaze dropped slowly to her lips, so full and lovely, begging to be kissed. I couldn't remember ever finding anyone so attractive before.

Without thinking about rejection, I said, "I think you might be the most beautiful person I've ever met, Cara. Inside and out, y'know? You're just . . . perfect."

"I was thinking the same thing about you." She smiled. My lips immediately mirrored hers. When she squeezed my hand this time, it was playful. "Thanks, by the way. For understanding about moms and craziness and whatnot."

"No problem." I dropped my gaze to our hands, but on the way, I couldn't help noticing how low the V-neck of her shirt dipped, and couldn't ignore the curves underneath. Suddenly the air felt very warm.

Devon's words echoed in my memory. *"Watch your step."*

Panic filled me—mostly because I didn't want to die at the hands of my girlfriend's brother, who was also my friend now, I guessed. And I hadn't really established the fact that I wanted Cara as my girlfriend in any official capacity, which meant that this could end up becoming a random hookup in action—something I definitely knew wouldn't fly with Devon. "So . . . I know you said he's been kind of distant, but . . . Devon seems pretty protective of you."

"My life is none of Devon's business." She stood and gave my hand a tug, nodding toward the front door of her house. "Come on. I wanna show you my room."

Suddenly I didn't give two shits about Devon or his opinions. I followed her inside and up the stairs, ignoring the mounds of religious paraphernalia that decorated the living room walls. Plaques featuring the seven deadly sins, a large framed list of the Ten Commandments, and enough crosses and dead Jesuses to choke a horse. A weird horse who liked eating religious junk. Probably one from small-town Michigan.

There was no sign of Martha, but I kept my footfalls as quiet as possible, just in case. Something told me that no parent—even a whackadoo like her—dreamed of the day a boy snuck into their daughter's bedroom.

The walls of Cara's room were covered in posters—mostly bands, but a few horror flicks—and behind the posters I could see she'd painted the walls a dark purple. Amid the posters were a few gravestone rubbings. A black, ornate vanity sat near the window, and across the room stood a matching, overstuffed bookcase. And there . . . at the center of the room . . . was a queen-sized bed to match. A bed. Cara's bed. Where she slept. Possibly naked.

Lying on top of her purple velvet duvet were her Tarot cards. She'd apparently been doing a reading for herself, as three cards lay faceup on the bed: the High Priestess, the Lovers, and the Magician. My eyes lingered on the card in the middle, and Cara's words echoed in my memory: *These three cards, from left to right, represent your past, your present, and your future.* The Lovers card was sitting in the present position. I sat on the edge of the mattress and pretended to look around, disinterested. "So . . . what do you want to do?"

Cara smirked. "Is that a line?"

"It might be. Is it working?" I cocked an eyebrow at her, trying my damnedest to be charming.

Cara moved closer and sat next to me on the bed. The

mattress sank down slightly and every cell in my body screamed in bliss that I could now say I'd been on a bed with this girl. Even if we hadn't done anything. Even if we never did.

She leaned closer and whispered in my ear, her hot breath tickling my skin. "Kiss me. Like you kissed me in the rain."

I didn't breathe, didn't hesitate, didn't give her even a microsecond to rethink her words. I pressed my lips to hers and we fell back on the bed, our mouths moving, our tongues exploring. I dared to put my hand on her waist, and she didn't push me away, so I slid it under her shirt and up her rib cage. She moaned softly, the way she had that day, the way I wanted her to moan again. Just to be sure it hadn't been a creation of my imagination. Just to relive the feeling that her moan had sent through me.

The lace on her bra was softer than I'd imagined. Softer than the sensation of her fingers gliding over my back. Softer than the feeling of her skin on my skin. Softer than my palm pressing anxiously against the lace itself. The tiny gold cross that hung around her neck gleamed in the low light, like sin coming out of the shadows. I kissed her hard on the mouth, feeling her heart race under my hands. Mine was racing, too. Mostly out of want, but partially out of fear. What if she didn't like the way I kissed? What if everything I was doing was wrong, and she never wanted me to do any of it ever again? I shut that inner critic up and placed a kiss on her chin, her neck, her collarbone. She moaned softly and tugged at my T-shirt until I sat up and removed it. I don't know where I threw it. I didn't care. She could take my clothes, my soul, my everything. As long as she didn't stop kissing me, touching me the way I needed her to. Gently, I caught her left hand in mine and placed a soft peck on her inner wrist. I moved up her arm, tasting her skin slightly on my lips, hungering for more, but afraid to press the issue without express permission. When I reached her shoulder, Cara caught my eye. Placing a hand gently on my chest, she pushed me back and sat up.

It was over now, this thing that had never really begun. Frustration and doubt and disappointment filled me, and I couldn't help wondering what I'd done wrong.

Then Cara slipped her shirt off over her head, dropping it to the floor. She beckoned me to her with a crook of her finger as she lay back on the bed with a smile that said that I'd had it all wrong. I was fine being wrong. I could always be wrong. So long as we kept kissing, kept touching, kept taking off our clothes, I could be more wrong than any man had ever been.

I didn't know if what I was feeling was love. It might have been. It might have been hormones, or even temporary insanity. I just knew that when Cara was around, I felt right.

When Cara looked at me, I felt like I mattered.

"Wait," she whispered, and I immediately paused. When a girl says "wait," you wait. Especially if she's letting you touch her in a way that makes your heart rattle the way that mine was rattling inside my chest.

For a moment, I thought that she'd changed her mind about what we were doing, but then she moved to her night-stand and opened the drawer. She placed her hand inside and when she withdrew it, my breath caught in my throat for a moment. Cara was holding a condom.

This shit just got real.

Cara returned to the bed and straddled my lap, facing me. She dropped the condom on the bed beside us and kissed me hard, sliding her hands down my chest, my stomach. With every inch, I thought for sure that I was going to explode. Mostly from happiness. In a bold move, I slid my hands around her back, my fingertips brushing the clasp there. Pinching the fabric, I felt one hook give way. I couldn't believe this was really happening.

"YOU'RE GONNA BURN!"

Shit.

Cara's eyes opened wide with shock and my attention shot immediately to the now-open door. Martha stood there, filling the frame. In the low light she looked like a giant banshee, her nightclothes billowing out from her in the soft breeze from the window. Her mouth was open wide as she shouted; her spindly arm raised with one long finger pointed accusingly right at me. She smacked her lips together, as if tasting the air. Then she spoke in a low growl that sent a shudder through my core. "You, boy. You're gonna burn."

I don't know how I got out from under Cara without knocking her to the floor. Or how I made it across the room and out the window. I was sliding down the porch roof, shingles scraping against my palms, the night air raising goose bumps on my bare chest, before I realized that I was outside. Something was stuck to my skin, so I peeled it off and dropped it to the ground. As it fluttered toward the front lawn, I recognized it as a Tarot card. The Lovers. The irony didn't escape me.

Still scrambling, I reached the edge of the porch, planted my right hand, and swung over, dropping to the ground and breaking into a sprint. Behind me, drifting out the window, Martha's declaration echoed. "You're gonna buuuuuuuuurn! Yoooouuuu'rrrre gooooonnaaaaa buuuuuuurrrrrrnn!"

As I ran for home, the wind blew my hair back from my forehead. Beads of sweat dripped from my skin. My lungs were on fire, and for a moment, I thought that Martha had been right. I was burning, burning up from the sinful deeds I'd been coaxing her daughter into.

I didn't know what would happen the next time I saw Martha, but I was relieved that I'd gotten out of there right away. I hoped that Martha would be directing all of her anger at the boy in her daughter's bedroom, rather than at her daughter. I hoped Cara wasn't dead right now, or grounded for as long as she could be contained. Maybe I wouldn't get to see her for a few months. Maybe we were over. I didn't know. All I knew was that my grandmother's house had never been a more welcome sight.

I reached the door breathless, and when I opened it, I found my father there, midnight snack in hand. My mouth dried completely, and any explanation that I could have offered him evaporated into the air between us. Just as I was about to brush past him without a word, he chuckled and said, "So . . . still seeing that Cara girl, son?"

I grinned. Sometimes my dad was all right. "Yeah, Dad. You could say that."

I headed straight to my room, and every step I took filled me with guilt. I'd left Cara without even an apology. Just left her there, with her crazy mother shrieking. I hoped she'd find a way to forgive me. And that I'd find a way back to her as soon as possible.

chapter 9

I'm pretty sure that nice guys call a girl after they fool around. So, since I spent the next three days rearranging my bedroom and actively avoiding the outside world, I guess you could say that I wasn't a nice guy. But in my defense, as much as I'd enjoyed being on her bed—oh god, being on her bed—the whole experience with Cara had freaked me out a little. Not that I'd ever admit to that in a court of law.

Unfortunately, the longer I waited, the weirder it was going to be the next time I saw her. And I couldn't stay at home forever.

The corner store in town was probably one of the most

miserable little markets known to mankind, but it was just about all Spencer had in the way of places to buy caffeine. The glass door had been covered with stickers over the years, and it was pretty clear that the owner never bothered to remove old advertisements before applying new ones. Right next to an Xbox sticker promoting the latest flavor of Mountain Dew was a Dr Pepper ad from who knows when saying that the girl with feathered bangs in the ad was a Pepper. Liar, I thought. You're not a Pepper. You're just some stupid girl advertising soda. Crappy soda, at that.

The inside of the shop was just as run-down as the outside. There were two aisles: one for booze, the other for candy, cigarettes, and candy cigarettes. In case there was any doubt about what the good citizens of Spencer did in their leisure time.

I grabbed a Mountain Dew (because advertising works . . . although I still wasn't a damn Pepper) and set it on the counter by the cash register. Even though I'd drunk enough water to drown every fish in the reservoir over the past few days, my mouth felt like sandpaper. My grandmother had Dad and me cleaning out and organizing her garage now, and my dad had this strange idea that consuming mass quantities of H_2O would be enough to combat the intense heat of a Michigan summer. Obviously, Dad didn't understand much about staying cool, literally or metaphorically. Or, you know, saying no to his mother.

The old man behind the counter reeked of tobacco and something else, too, something just as sick.

I'd heard about how dogs can pick up on cancer in their owners, and how people train them to smell the sickness inside. Now I'm not saying this old man had cancer, although maybe he did. I just knew that something was wrong with him, and I hoped that whatever it was, it wouldn't be wrong with me someday.

He coughed into a handkerchief and said, "Dollah fiddy."

Assuming that this was some kind of monetary amount, I pulled my wallet from my back pocket. The bell above the door jingled as the door opened. Lane stepped inside, acknowledging me with something between a scowl and a "'sup" nod before heading to the candy/cigarettes/candy cigarettes aisle.

He grabbed a Snickers bar and came up to the counter beside me. I started to say, *What, no drinking and driving today?* But decided it was better not to engage. I could see Holly outside in his car, and I hoped like hell he wasn't going to raise the subject of me hanging out with his little posse again, because frankly, I didn't have it in me to say no politely. For a moment, I thought I'd lucked out and he-who'd-been-named-after-a-small-road had come down with a terrible case of laryngitis, but then, like an idiot, I made eye contact. It was all over. "Hey, Stephen. What are you up to?"

"Buying a Mountain Dew?" I had no idea why it came out like a question. I guess I was in awe of his observational abilities.

He nodded and glanced at the bottle on the counter, as if to confirm that I was indeed purchasing a caffeinated beverage.

"I heard you were hanging out with that Cara girl."

My jaw tightened. I didn't like the way he said *hanging out*. "Yeah. What of it?"

Lane shrugged, a smart-ass look on his face. "Nothin'. She's just kind of a sk—"

I had a pretty good idea what he was about to say. I also had a pretty good idea that Lane was about to get punched in the face.

But then the bell above the door jingled, and Lane went quiet. I turned to see Scot and Cam step inside. At first they didn't notice me. Cam was texting as he walked, barely looking where he was going. After he put his phone in his pocket, he glanced my way and smiled. "Hey Stephen. What's up?"

"Not much. Just trying not to die from the heat. You know."

Scot chuckled. "If you think this is hot, just wait till the humidity really kicks in. This is nothing."

As if I needed another reason to loathe Michigan sum-
mers. But it felt good to joke about them for a change.

Cam and Scot headed for the cooler. They looked at what
was inside for a moment before Cam called to the guy behind
the counter, "Got any Diet Pepsi?"

The man narrowed his eyes and grumbled, "If it ain't in
da coolah, I ain't got it."

Scot shrugged and tugged Cam out the door again. On
their way, both offered me "later" nods and smiles, rolling
their eyes at the guy behind the counter, as if the three of us
were in on the same joke. Register Guy snorted and before
the door could even close all the way, he said, "Fags gotta
keep their girlish figures, I s'pose."

Lane laughed like it was the funniest thing he ever
heard. I froze. An angry heat crawled up my neck to my face.
I was insulted on Scot and Cam's behalf, but I'd be lying if I
said I was surprised. This was exactly the kind of bullshit I
expected from a town like Spencer. I tossed a glare at Lane
and then threw it at the old man. "Doesn't it bother you that
you're furthering the stereotype of closed-minded hicks?"

They both just stared at me like I was an alien, until I
said, "Those guys are my friends. Lane, you're an ass."

Without an ounce of shame or regret, Lane scoffed right
in my face. The old man leaned forward and in a gravelly
voice said, "Well, if you're so bothered by it, Sally, why don't

you hike up your skirt and follow 'em on outta here?"

In my mind, I wished something horrible on the old man. Something I couldn't picture specifically, but horrible nonetheless.

Suddenly, the man behind the register began to cough. But he didn't *just* cough. His entire thin, aged body racked with such violent spasms as he coughed that I thought he might die right then and there. The old man—still coughing—stretched out a hand so I could presumably put a dollah fiddy in his palm. Another cough sent his hand straight into the bottle of Mountain Dew, knocking it to the floor. The plastic bottle hit the tile with a thud and Mountain Dew burst out of the seam around the cap, spraying everywhere. Dropping my wallet on the counter, I bent down and grabbed it, covering the busted seam with my hand and trying to stop the sugary onslaught.

When I came back up, I half expected to find the old man dead on the counter. But no such luck. He wheezed one last wheeze, then he took a deep breath and just stared. "You still gotta pay for dat."

I stared back at the old man. He had to be kidding me.

Holding out his hand once again, he said, "Dollah fiddy."

Reluctantly, I reached for my wallet on the counter. But it was gone.

The bell above the door jingled and I watched as Lane

dashed outside, my wallet in hand. To say I was pissed didn't even begin to cover it. I ran out the door as fast as I could, but it was too late. Lane's car peeled out, Holly laughing her head off in the passenger seat, and I was left standing there, breathing in the smell of exhaust and burnt tires, not knowing what I was supposed to do.

"You left me!" The words came suddenly, and so did the shove on my shoulder as Cara whipped around to face me. She was wearing my shirt—the one I'd abandoned on her bedroom floor. It looked incredibly sexy on her, and I wondered if I would ever get it back again. But mostly I didn't care. Smacking me on my arm, her eyes wide with incredulity, she said, "I can't believe you! It's bad enough you just left me there with my crazy mother, but then you don't even stop by or call or anything? For three whole days!"

"So . . . you're mad?"

Cara rolled her eyes. "No."

I sighed in relief. At the same time, a smirk settled on her lips. Her perfectly kissable lips. "I just can't believe you left like that. I didn't know what to think. I've never had a guy run out on me before. You should've seen the look on your face. Priceless."

I was immediately tempted to ask just how many times she'd had a guy in her room like that, but I managed to resist. It wasn't any of my business. Besides, Spencer was a small town. Going by math alone, how many guys could there possibly have been? "I'll have you know your mother can be a very intimidating woman."

Cara nodded, her voice dripping with what I hoped was sarcasm. "Yeah, she frequently scares boys out my window and down the roof."

Screw resistance.

"What boys?"

Grinning, she shoved me again, but lightly this time. I had the undeniable urge to pull her closer and kiss her throat. As she turned and headed down the sidewalk, she said, "You are so aggravating. Why did I sneak out to see you?"

"Does that mean no more grope-fests?" She rolled her eyes at me over her shoulder, but I stood my ground. My shaky, hormonal-boy ground. "No, seriously."

"Maybe. We'll see. For now, I'm still grounded. So I'd better get home." She stopped on the sidewalk, turning back to face me, and shrugged. "For a few more days at least. Till Martha forgets what she walked in on."

"I know I won't forget it." It sounded like a line—maybe it was—but I meant what I'd said. I'd never forget the way that Cara's skin had felt against mine, or the way that she'd made my heart race. Some moments in life were etched into your memory. Some were burned into your soul.

"You're sweet." She stood there on the sidewalk, looking conflicted about leaving. She said, "I'd better get the hell out of here before I kiss you again."

She turned, and as she walked away at a good clip, I called after her, still hopeful, "That would be a bad thing?"

She kept on walking.

A few hours later, I found myself bored and alone in the oh-so-exciting downtown area of Spencer, Michigan, where the top summertime activities consisted of people watching and car watching. And there weren't that many cars on the road. After returning home to borrow a few bucks from my dad, cursing Lane the whole time, I'd finally grabbed that Mountain Dew (dollah fiddy), along with a bag of Doritos (dollah turdy), and parked myself on a bench across the street from the gas station. I'd swiped Devon's journal from my nightstand and shoved it in my back pocket, but couldn't even muster the energy to flip through its pages. Like I said, I was bored. Too bored to even entertain myself. But not bored enough to hang out with my grandmother or my dad. I don't think anyone in the history of man has ever been that bored.

"What's goin' on, dude?" Markus plopped down on the bench beside me, just as I was crumpling up my empty Doritos bag.

I offered him a shrug and washed back the Doritos taste

with a swig of pop. "Not much. Just sitting here. Wishing I was somewhere else."

"You've basically described the entire adolescent experience." He chuckled, and then followed my gaze across the street. "Seriously, what's up?"

"I don't know. I'm still trying to figure things out around here. What do people do for fun in Spencer? I mean, I've been sitting here for twenty minutes, watching these old men across the street, and they haven't done anything. They've only moved to use the restroom or grab another cold one."

"So let me get this straight. You've been sitting on this bench for half an hour, staring at some old men in front of the gas station. And you're wondering why they don't seem to have a life?" Markus raised a sharp eyebrow at me. "Somebody please call the irony police."

"Okay. Point taken. But what about the kids?" I gestured around at the empty sidewalks. "It's a sunny summer day and no one's outside. It's me, you, and the old men. And they just sit there. Every day. For hours."

"They're not just sitting there. They're waiting."

"For what?"

"Just . . . waiting." He shrugged, his eyes on the old men. "Since the auto parts factory two towns over closed down, it's all most people in Spencer can do. Wait for the factory to reopen, or for a new one to open in its place. And in the meantime, wait for the unemployment checks to show up in the mail. Times are pretty tough for everybody right now."

"That I do know." Sweat rolled down my forehead and I wiped it away with my arm, wondering if there would ever be a break in the heat. "But I don't know, it just seems like no one is really doing anything about it around here. It's like everybody's given up. Is that bad luck, or is this place just cursed?"

"If you have nothing better to do, why not go see a movie or something?"

"Can't. No cash. My dad is as broke as everybody else, and that douche bag Lane stole my wallet." I'd thought about reporting it to the cops, but really, this was between Lane and me. Tattling on him to the authorities was no way to show him what a dick move he'd made. Egging his car, on the other hand . . .

"Did he, now?" Markus grew quiet for a moment, his demeanor chilled. Then he slid his thumbs in his front pockets and shrugged. "Don't worry about Lane. The boys and I will take care of it."

Right. Take care of it. As if they were the mafia of small-town Michigan or something.

I watched as one of the old men across the street nudged another and nodded in my direction. I chuckled. "It *would* be kind of funny if they were staring at me wondering why I don't do anything all day. An endless loop of 'what the hell,' y'know?"

"You really are sad here, aren't you, Stephen?"

A heavy sigh escaped me. "Yeah, to be honest. Hanging out in the Playground is great. You and the rest of the guys are great. Devon's great. Cara is . . ."

"Hot."

I skipped over that commentary. One: I really didn't want anybody but me noticing how hot Cara was, and two: I didn't want anybody noticing that I'd noticed how hot Cara was. "But I still can't figure out if I'm here for the long haul or not. And I still don't feel like I fit in either way."

"Who cares about fitting in? Fitting in is overrated. The important thing is you don't waste what time you do have sitting here judging everybody else." We exchanged looks. Markus held up his hands in self-defense. "I'm just saying. Who gives a shit what they do, what you do, the endless loop or whatever? Just do *something* and screw the rest."

I sighed again, but this time with fewer dramatics. "Another valid point."

"You keeping score?"

"I might be."

"For the record," Markus said, "Devon might be, too."

I shot him a glance. "What do you mean?"

He looked around and lowered his voice, as if someone might be trying to listen in on our conversation. "Cara,
dude. You've gotta be real careful when it comes to Devon's
sister. When I first moved here, I made a comment about the
royal hotness that is our fearless leader's sister and he hit me
so hard it dislocated my jaw."

"Damn," was what I said, but the word inside my mind
started with an *F*. A big, totally screwed *F*.

Markus was looking at me with the air of a man speaking to a death row inmate. "Yeah. So just be careful, okay?
Cuz if you hurt her, Devon will cut your balls off."

"Funny, those are the exact words he used with me,
too." I tried to laugh it off like I really did think it was
funny, but I suddenly felt like my shirt was too tight around
the neck. I was very much in need of a subject change. "So,
Markus. Where'd you move here from, anyway?"

"Atlanta." When he said the name of his former home, a
look of longing crossed his eyes. Moving here clearly hadn't
been his preference, either. "Hotlanta, if ya like. My mom
moved here for a boyfriend, but he's out of the picture now."

"You don't have an accent. Where's your southern drawl?"

"Not everyone from Georgia sounds like they're from
the country. There you go, judging again." He nudged me
with his elbow as he stood. "Come on. I'll show you what I do
to stay entertained around here."

He turned right and I followed him, dropping my empty Doritos bag and half-empty Mountain Dew bottle in one of the three public trash cans in Spencer as we rounded the corner onto Water Street.

"Does what we're going to see involve Devon and the other guys?"

"Not this time."

"So what about tonight? You guys hanging out at the Playground like always?"

"You know it. We hang out there every night." He looked at me like he was daring me to judge him, too. "And frankly, we've been wondering where you've been."

I shrugged, forgoing a whine about my grandmother's endless list of chores, which would have been only half true. "Just been kind of tired. But I'm up for it tonight."

"Ah. Can't do it tonight. We're busy."

"You're busy? Or we're busy, meaning I'm expected to attend something else?"

"Look, it's private business with the rest of the gang, okay? I can't say any more than that. Hell, I've already said too much. Devon would kick my ass if he knew." Markus ran a hand through his hair, brushing it away from his eyes. There was a nervous edge to his movement.

"He can't kick your ass for not telling me anything. On the other hand, if you *want* to tell me what's up, I promise I won't tell. I thought I was supposed to be in on all the secrets after the other night anyway."

Markus flinched.

"Just . . . not tonight, okay? And stop asking so many damn questions." He sounded irritated, which was strange considering I was the one being ditched. Had Devon found out about me and Cara, and now wanted to plan exactly how they were going to kill me? He knew. He had to know. Of course he knew. He was Devon.

As we rounded the corner near the movie theater, Markus nodded to a small, square building up ahead of us. The sign on the front was practically falling apart, its paint so faded that the words *Spencer Library* were difficult to read. "Here we are."

I blinked at him for several seconds. It wasn't that I didn't like books. I totally got the whole pull-to-fiction-for-escapism thing. I'd just kind of been under the impression that he was taking me somewhere seriously cool. Like maybe into the attic of the mansion to hunt for ghosts or some shit. I don't know. Anything would have been better than the nondescript building I was staring at. "This is how you pass the time? At some run-down, dusty library?"

At Markus's proud nod, I said, "I'm going back to the gas station."

Markus caught me by the arm and tugged me toward

the library. "Hey, it's better than staring at old men all day. Besides, I think you'll be interested in what I have to show you. Come on."

Markus looked quickly in both directions before we went in, almost like he was making sure we weren't being followed. That, more than anything, finally caught my interest.

The inside of the library was far better taken care of than the outside, even if it was a little overstuffed with books. Off to the right there was a small grouping of four desks, with four giant, ancient desktop computers. The walls of the library were decorated with a "tasteful" blend of local artistry and posters encouraging people to read. From behind a tall desk to the left, a woman's head popped up. She had graying hair and a pleasant smile, and wore small rectangular spectacles on the end of her nose. A thin pink sweater was draped over her shoulders, and dangling from the ends of her glasses was a beaded chain, shiny and every color you could think of. She looked, to put it plainly, the way I'd hoped my grandmother would look when we pulled into town. Warm, inviting. Kind. "Oh, hello, Markus. I thought I'd be seeing you soon. Heading downstairs?"

Markus smiled and guided me around several tall piles of books. The place didn't appear messy so much as organized in a way that only the librarian could understand.

"You know it, Ms. Rose. This is Stephen, by the way."

Ms. Rose gave an absentminded wave. "A pleasure to have you, Stephen. Enjoy yourselves. Let me know if you need help finding anything."

We came to a narrow, metal staircase that spiraled down into the floor. As we descended into darkness, my grip on the handrail tightened in apprehension. Markus hit a button on the wall as we reached the bottom of the stairs. The lights flickered on, and I gasped. Though the room upstairs had had a sense of order to it, the basement level was utter chaos. Along each of the four walls were large shelves, stretching from ceiling to floor. Each shelf was stuffed full of books, newspapers, and boxes of microfiche film. In front of the shelves were piles—almost too many to count—of books and newspapers. A heavy layer of dust covered everything, striking a sad chord inside me. I hated to see so much history forgotten. I looked to Markus, who nodded, as if he could see my thoughts written all over my face and agreed with my assessment completely. He placed his left hand on my shoulder and then swept his right arm out in front of us, gesturing to the room in all its dusty glory. "These, my friend, are what's affectionately known as the stacks."

Nodding with appreciation and more than a touch of wonder, I said, "Appropriate."

Markus led me farther into the room, and just around a

large pile of newspapers that almost matched me in height, there was a break in the mess. Two leather wingback chairs sat at the center of the room, atop an old oriental rug. Between the chairs was a small table, and on top of that was a lamp that reminded me very much of one my dad had purchased for my mom's birthday a few years ago. She'd described it as "art deco" or some such thing, but when I'd looked at it, all I'd seen was old metal and bubbles of glass. Still. Seeing this lamp now sent a sentimental shiver up my spine.

Markus stood by the chair on the right and looked appreciatively around the room. "What you're looking at is the history of Spencer since before Spencer was. Every newspaper article, every book, every little printed snippet of this town that exists lives here. My favorites are the piles by the chairs. Those are all the screwed-up stuff that's happened in this town over the years. During the—"

"—bad times?"

He blinked at my interruption, and it was clear from his expression that this had been precisely what he was going to say. I wondered if such thorough documentation was common in towns this small, but doubted it. Hell, it probably wasn't all that common in big towns, either. "So why are you showing this to me exactly?"

Markus shrugged. "Because it's entertaining. Reading through some of the stuff in here, some of the scandals, some of the beliefs and stories . . . it's just cool is all. But if you'd rather stare at old men or watch paint dry . . ."

"Where should I start?"

He sighed, and I got the feeling he was resisting the urge to strangle me. He said, "It's like a big lake, Stephen. You just hold your breath and dive in."

After a glimpse around the room, I sat hard in the chair on the left, half expecting a cloud of dust to fill the air. The chair was surprisingly cozy, and amazingly clean, considering the state of its surroundings. Sitting next to it was a stack of newspapers with far less dust on them than I'd seen on any of the surrounding books. I grabbed a couple of papers off the top and started scanning the pages. The date on the first copy of the *Spencer Gazette* that I'd grabbed was October 31, 1898. On the front page, in big, bold letters, was a headline I couldn't miss: TOWN FOUNDER TURNED MURDER SUSPECT!

Scanning the article, I gathered what had to be the most interesting—and twisted—thing I'd heard about Spencer's history yet. Apparently, William Spencer's daughter had been found dead on the outskirts of town one evening. She'd been strangled, and all evidence had pointed to her father as the only suspect. The article delved into details of his arrest, but ended with more questions than answers. It made me wonder what could possibly cause a successful businessman to turn on his own child. He must have gone nuts. Maybe it was the pressure of having the economy of an entire village balanced on his shoulders. Whatever the reason, the story left a sick feeling in my stomach, so I moved on to the next paper in the pile.

Markus sat in the other chair, perusing a paper of his own. He kept looking over at me, though, and I couldn't shake the feeling that he was waiting for something.

The date at the top of the next newspaper was September 6, 1962. After JFK asked not what our country could do for us, but before MLK had a dream. The first few pages focused on the major headlines that week, but the third page dug into local news. Apparently, there'd been a ragin' bake sale on the corner of Main Street and Water Street that week, and a pound of ground beef was on sale for only thirty-four cents. But at the bottom right corner, ten bold words caught my eye, and I immediately wondered why this headline had not been placed up front and center, as it seemed like it would have been important news at the time, even outside of Spencer. The headline read: PASSENGER TRAIN PLUMMETS INTO RESERVOIR, KILLING THIRTY-ONE SPENCER RESIDENTS.

The article listed names, but not a lot of details. The train had apparently been on its way to Spencer from the next town over, a daily occurrence that had brought many factory and mill workers to and from the larger town. It derailed without known cause, devastating the small town.

And with good reason. When your town is composed of only eight hundred or so souls, losing thirty-one of them in one fell swoop is pretty terrible. As I reached the end of the article, I found myself absurdly interested in what the reporter had to say about the accident. *"Long black feathers were found at the scene, causing this reporter to wonder if the myth of the Winged Ones is merely town lore, or a horrific reality that we all must face."*

I sat back in the chair, chewing my bottom lip absently. I pulled Devon's journal from my back pocket and flipped to a section in the middle. On one page was a scribbled drawing of a man being torn to bits by a giant beak. On another a child was being clutched in large, sharp claws and carried openmouthed and screaming into the foreboding night sky. In big, bold letters on yet another page, he'd written a single word. *Justice.*

I turned the pages, searching for a drawing I remembered seeing the last time I'd looked at the journal. Toward the back, I found it. The bridge that Devon's friend Bobby had dove off before he drowned. The train on the tracks, the engine car derailed. The people falling out of the windows, their faces twisted in agony. And above them all, as if just barely captured before they fled the scene, the giant, feathered wings of the Winged Ones, terrorizing the train and pushing it over the edge.

Last time I'd looked at it, Devon's journal had seemed like a brilliant piece of fiction based on a small town's superstitions. It had seemed like a book. A creative outlet. Right?

But there was that strange feather in the cemetery, and tall tales this crazy surely came from *somewhere*.

What if Devon truly believed the Winged Ones were real?

chapter 10

A few things could be said for the way my grandmother's house usually smelled, and none of them were very pleasant. But as I strolled up the driveway, hungry for dinner, smells that shouldn't have been coming from her house definitely were. Delicious, nose-filling, Mexican-food smells that made me feel almost happy I was going inside. My dad's Beetle was gone, so apparently, my grandmother could cook. Who knew?

At the stove, my grandmother was busy stirring something in a pot, her back to me. I cleared my throat to let her know I was in the room, and she bristled. Clearly, after two weeks in the same house, we still weren't friends. "Smells good. Is that dinner? I love Mexican food."

She didn't respond, just kept stirring whatever was in the pot. Then, as if fully embracing her position as Evil Old Hag, she tapped her wooden spoon clean on the edge of the pot and set it on a spoon rest that was shaped like a goose looking over its shoulder. The spoon rested on the goose's hindquarters—something that didn't exactly instill my faith in tonight's meal, whatever the smells. My grandmother turned to look at me, wiping her hands on her white-and-blue-checkered apron. There was an expression on her face I didn't recognize. She looked almost . . . happy. "It's your father's favorite, too. I've been cooking this for him since he was two."

I sat there stunned for a moment. Not only was it already the most pleasant conversation we'd engaged in to date, but also she'd told me something about my dad I hadn't known. I always thought he preferred Italian, what with the way he used to drool over the very mention of my mom's lasagna. Either my grandmother was wrong or my dad had been lying to one of them.

A memory curled up in the back of my mind, warm and safe and pleasant. My mom, standing in our kitchen in Denver. She was wearing that ugly flower-covered apron that she loved so much, moving boiled lasagna noodles from the strainer in the sink to the glass pan on the counter. My dad had come up behind her, slipping his hands over her hips. I'd walked into the room to ask a question, but as I turned to walk out again, to leave them alone in that couple-only moment, Dad had spoken softly into my mother's ear. She'd giggled in such a normal way, and he'd said, "You know lasagna's my favorite."

I pushed the memory away and looked at my grandmother, missing the family I'd once had more than ever. It was a start, this conversation. It was something, at least.

My grandmother nodded, as if she was thinking the same thing. "Now go wash up. Dinner is in five minutes."

I offered a hesitant smile in return and made my way down the hall toward the bathroom. As I walked, I caught a funky smell, and realized it was me. So I stepped into my bedroom to change my shirt and reapply some deodorant. These face-melting Michigan summer days were going to be the death of me or the people around me. As I pulled a fresh T-shirt over my head, I furrowed my brow and looked around the room. Something was off, but I couldn't pinpoint what. Then it hit me. The photograph of my mom that had been sitting on my nightstand wasn't there. Instead there was just space, just emptiness.

Thinking that it must have fallen, I searched the floor around the table, but found nothing. It also hadn't been accidentally kicked under my bed. As I stood there, that little voice in the back of my head—the one that usually has a pretty good idea of what's going on—whispered that the only way the photograph could have disappeared was if someone took it. And I had a sinking feeling I knew who was capable of that.

I tried to keep my temper under control. My grandmother had set the table for three, and was folding her apron when I came into the kitchen. She looked at me with a challenge in her eyes that told me that she knew exactly why I was so angry. I glanced up and confirmed that Mom's teapot was also missing. Then I took a breath before speaking and blew it out slowly, so that my head had less of a chance of exploding. "Do you know what happened to the photograph of my mom that was on my nightstand? It's missing."

I was fully prepared for her to lie, to tell me she hadn't seen it. *What picture? Why, fiddle-dee-dee, I have no idea to what photograph you are referring.* Or some such crap. What I was not prepared for were the words she released into the air between us, and how they filled that space with a thick layer of combustible gas.

"Some lessons in this world come easy, and some come hard. I had hoped that this one would come easy enough for you, but with your father needing the same education, that doesn't seem to be the case. So it falls on me to bring a little hard wisdom into your life." Her thin eyebrows seemed sharp in the afternoon light, and she raised one starkly at me as she stared me down. I'd had no idea that a woman of her size could be so intimidating until that moment. "Your mother is dead."

In an instant, my chest ached and every bit of air left my lungs in a horrified gasp.

My mother was dead. I had pushed her to the back of my mind, ignored her, and even said she was no longer my mother. And now, she was gone.

My grandmother nodded, as if satisfied that she'd given her statement enough time to sink in. She continued, "There is physical death and then there is spiritual death, and while her body might still be with us, for all practical purposes, the woman who brought you into this world is deceased. And when a person is deceased, it is up to the living to go on living. I have packed all of those mementos up and placed them in storage. When the time comes that you and your father have properly grieved, they will be returned to you."

My jaw tensed. I could feel my hands begin to shake, but kept my eyes locked on hers. What a sick, horrible thing to say. If anyone were dead, I wished in that moment that it was the woman standing in front of me.

"Give it back." The furious heat crawling up my neck and face was intense—so much so that I felt like I was fully engulfed in flames. "Give my photograph back. *Now*."

Not at all fazed by the unseen flames before her, my grandmother remained calm and cool. "No."

She wasn't going to budge. She'd stolen from me, insulted my mom, tried to control me and my dad, and made my life miserable from the moment I met her. She wasn't a grandmother. She wasn't even a decent person. If I could've shot lasers from my eyes at that point, I would have. "You're just an old . . ."

But I couldn't say it. I couldn't get the word out of my mouth. I couldn't say it even if she was being one. Because she was my grandmother, even if she was a total—

"Bitch?" Her upper lip twitched, but she said the word like she owned it. Clearly, she had been called that once or twice in her lifetime. But never by her grandson. Because I was the only one she had, like it or not. "Yes, I am. But at least I am in my faculties enough to care for my family and not get locked away in some nuthouse."

I took a quick step toward her and lowered my voice. "Maybe you should be."

"And maybe we'd all be better off if your mother was truly dead."

It was the first moment in my life that I had ever seriously considered punching an old lady.

"What's going on in here?" My dad was standing by the

front door. I didn't know when he'd come in or how long he'd been listening to our heated exchange.

I just knew that he was going to flip when he heard what his mother had done, what his mother had said. And then, after putting her in her place, he would tell me to toss our stuff in the backseat of the Beetle so we could get the hell out of Dodge. "She stole my picture of Mom. She took Mom's teapot and who knows what else. And she refuses to give them back! It's like she's trying to erase Mom from our lives!"

My father stood there, looking more meek and defeated than I had ever seen him. Slowly, he moved his gaze from me to his mother and back again. I was suddenly filled with the disappointing realization that when my mother was put away, my father had lost his spine. Grasping at strings of frayed hope, I said, "Dad? Did you know about this?"

With a final glance at his mother, my dad held his hands up toward me in a pleading gesture. His tone quieted, and the finality of that old bat's triumph settled in. She'd won. "I'm not saying that your grandmother's actions are warranted or well timed. But . . . maybe it's best that we do move forward with our lives, son. We can't cling to the past forever."

I wanted to say something, but before I could, Dad added, "Stephen . . . I just got back from an interview with the power company outside of town. I got a job offer. Taking it means that we stay here, and that your mom will have to stay at the facility in Denver. It's just the best place for her, son."

Without another word, I walked out the door, slamming it behind me as hard as I could. Before I said something to my father that I might one day regret.

I wandered the outskirts of town for several hours, having bitter conversations in my head. I didn't want to be around people, and I was in no state to see Cara, knowing that anything I did or said would only hurt anybody I ran into. What I really needed was to cool off, get wasted, and forget about my life for a while. Invitation or not.

After the sun sank below the horizon for the evening, I made my way to the Playground, where, just as I expected, I found Devon and the boys. Markus looked sheepish and maybe even a little alarmed to see me, but as far as I could tell, I wasn't interrupting anything special. Our fearless leader was dressed in black on black, his clothing once again reminding me of military regalia. Moonlight gleamed off the buttons on his jacket. Devon smiled when he saw me. "Somebody grab this man a bottle. Clearly, Stephen needs to get shitfaced."

I parked my ass on the ground and my back against a tall, rectangular stone. Devon took a spot beside me, on the same grave. It occurred to me that none of us ever remarked on the dead bodies that were decaying below our chosen hangout. We ignored death, pretending that it wasn't so close. But there it was. Just feet from us. Waiting.

Neither Devon nor I said anything for a good, long time. We passed a bottle of something green back and forth until the edges of the world blurred away. The boys were listening to music, but everyone seemed a little subdued tonight. They could all tell I was in a shitty mood, so they tread lightly and kept their distance from me. Everyone but Devon.

I emptied the bottle and stared at it in silence. Devon pulled something out of his back pocket and handed it to me. Turning the object over in my free hand, I was struck by disbelief, and had several questions that I couldn't put into words. He'd handed me my wallet. Flipping it open, I glanced at my license before nodding and shoving it in my back pocket.

"How did you get this?"

"Probably better not to ask."

"I thought I was part of the group now."

"I thought so, too. But we haven't seen you in a few days, Stephen. And you've been keeping a few secrets of your own, haven't you?"

All I could manage to say was, "Thanks for the wallet."

"So what's eating you tonight?" Devon looked at me, his

head tilted in curiosity. The moonlight made his bleach-blond hair seem to glow. That might've just been the liquor talking. "Something's obviously gnawing on your insides, Stephen. What is it?"

Snorting, I tossed the bottle I was holding and watched it land six feet in front of us. It rolled down a small, grassy mound and completed a half circle before coming to rest at the foot of a tombstone that was shaped like a cross. The moonlight cast a long, black shadow cross over the grass. "It's everything. It's this town. It's these people. It's this life."

Devon dropped his eyes to the ground for a brief moment before meeting my gaze with something that felt like respect. "It's not all that bad. You have me and the boys."

"True."

"We're soldiers in the same army, marching for a cause. And that cause is a just one." I couldn't help but notice, even in my inebriated state, that he failed to identify what that cause was. "Loyalty, Stephen. That's what we have to offer you. It's yours if you want it."

"I do."

"Plus . . ." He inhaled slowly through his nose, as if his next words would take considerable effort on his part. "Loath as I am to warm to the notion . . . you have Cara."

The sour look on Devon's face suggested he might have had a difficult time swallowing after saying that last sentence, but he didn't look as angry as I'd feared he would be. "Just so you know, we're not just screwing around, Devon. I really care about your sister."

"I know."

"How do you know?" I said. His answer had surprised me. I thought that Cara and I had been pretty good at keeping us a secret—at least from her brother. Either she'd told him, which seemed unlikely given the icy state of their relationship, or he was an even better spy than I realized.

"Nobody wants their balls cut off. Or worse." A small smile touched his lips as he twisted the cap off another bottle and passed it to me. "Now drink up. You look like you could still use a few swigs."

I took a healthy swallow, not minding the way the liquor burned my throat and stomach anymore. Some things you just get used to. Even bad things. "This town, man. This town. No offense, but I wish we'd never moved here."

He took the bottle from my hand and tilted his head back. Licking his lips, he handed it to me. His skin looked pale in the firelight. "What exactly bothers you about Spencer?"

"It's just . . . nothing." I groaned, so sick of everything. Even myself. "I hate my grandmother. And this place seems a lot like her. Old. Bitter. Stuck."

Devon chuckled. "You, my man, have this place pegged."

I wasn't convinced that his words had been meant to offer me any kind of comfort at all. It didn't matter, though. Nothing could comfort me at that moment. I was feeling angry and lost and restless and stupid. "Hey . . . Devon? I have a confession to make."

"Oh?"

I knew that what I was about to do was either incredibly smart or incredibly stupid. I also knew the only way to know which it was lay in Devon's reaction.

After swallowing another mouthful of the green stuff, I pulled his journal out of my back pocket and handed it to him.

One entry stuck out in my mind as I looked at him now—a confession from our fearless leader, apparently in his own words: *I fear them, but long for their approval. I seek them out, but loathe the notion of them doing the same to me. Still, they are real. More real than anything else here.*

His eyes lit up at first with surprise, then relief. Then the clouds rolled into his expression, darkening his demeanor like a storm.

"I found it. And I read it." My words were calm, but I felt like I should be running out of the Playground in a sprint of terror, leaving Devon behind. After a single heartbeat, I added, "Please don't kill me." I hoped I was kidding.

He turned the small journal over in his hands, stroking

the worn leather cover. The book obviously meant a lot to him. I felt bad that I hadn't returned it to him the moment that I learned he was its owner, its author, its artist. With his eyes on the journal, Devon spoke calmly. "This is a grievous offense, Stephen. This journal is private. I must admit . . . I'm not happy."

He clenched his jaw. "Most definitely not."

A shaky breath escaped my lungs. He'd just given me a pass for being involved with his sister. But something told me that the journal meant more to him than even her. "I didn't think you would be. But what's done is done, right?"

He nodded after a moment. What was done was done. My move to Spencer. My relationship with his sister. And now this. "I meant for you to find it. And to read it. But not for you to keep it so damn long."

Questions filled my mind, but I wasn't sure how to ask them. Before I could form the words, he said, "Did anything in particular catch your eye?"

I sat forward, holding his gaze. "Tell me more about the Winged Ones."

As the words left my lips, they caught the attention of the entire group, even though it had seemed that no one had been listening to us prior to that moment. The fun, it seemed, was over.

Devon spoke softly, not looking at anyone in particular,

his head tilted up as if he were speaking to the moon. "Stephen wants to know about the Winged Ones."

The gang was strangely quiet, the music had stopped, and it took Devon a moment to say anything else. "What do you want to know?"

I opted for the truth. "I guess . . . I mean, they're just a story, right? You don't seriously believe that a bunch of horror movie creatures control the fate of everybody in this town."

Lighting a clove cigarette, Devon stood. With the ease of a trained acrobat, he hopped up on the tallest tombstone in the cemetery and perched there. When I struggled to stand, largely thanks to the booze, Markus stepped closer and helped me up. He held his free arm close to his side. Upon closer inspection, I noticed that his wrist was swollen some. His words from earlier echoed in my skull. *"Devon would kick my ass if he knew."*

The rest of the boys crowded in, looking up at our fearless leader. After a brief nod at Markus, I followed suit.

"Spencer's belief in the Winged Ones stretches all the way back to the early 1800s, when half of the original settlers went out hunting one day, then came back to find their families missing. Blood and enormous black feathers lined the streets, but the people were gone without a trace. It was one of the bad times."

My heart skipped a beat.

"But that wasn't the only bad time. There are countless other tales. There was a class field trip in 1913 that simply disappeared while exploring a maple syrup farm on the edge of town, there was a kid in the seventies who disappeared after breaking into the mansion, and many, many more. People have been passing down tales of the Winged Ones as bedtime stories for as long as the town has existed. I was raised on them. Everyone here was. Except Markus. And you, of course." He inhaled on his cigarette and blew out, the smoke forming a foggy halo around his head. He was Saint Devon now. As the moniker entered my mind, he looked at me. Almost like he knew what I was thinking. "But there are other stories, too. Stories of good times, when the Winged Ones were appeased. And do you know how that happens, Stephen? It's said that the only way to appease their fury, the only way to make the bad times go away again . . . is by offering up a human sacrifice."

Silence surrounded me, surrounded us. No one breathed. Even the fire refused to crackle. My heartbeat thumped in my ears, the only sound over the sudden hush.

Finally, I said, "That's scary as shit." What a messed-up way to raise your kids, with the fear that monsters are real and might come devour them one day. Not for punishment or anything. Just because. I shook my head. "But still . . . do you really believe in the Winged Ones just because of some bedtime stories?"

Saint Devon shrugged. "People believe in a lot of things."

"Do you?" I repeated.

Markus, Cam, Scot, Nick, and Thorne all set their eyes on me then, and I knew that I was asking questions that weren't supposed to be asked.

The glow of Devon's cigarette ember put a strange light in his eyes—one that sent a shiver down my spine. "Why are you asking, Stephen? You've seen my notebook. You know what I believe."

Turning slowly, I looked at Markus. At Scot and Cam, Nick and Thorne. I could barely utter the question inside my mind. "Do all of you believe in them?"

None of them spoke, or even took the time to confer with one another before answering. Instead, they all nodded— even Markus.

From atop his story-time pedestal, Saint Devon flicked his clove cigarette onto the ground and, standing slowly, towering above us all, said, "Have another drink, Stephen. Markus and I will be sure to carry you home."

The tension broke and the revelry resumed, almost as if I'd never brought up the Winged Ones at all. But I wasn't fooled. I stood there on the edge of the group, wondering what the hell was happening to the small bubble of a world around me. Markus stepped over to me, took a swig from a bottle of his favorite, peach schnapps, then held it out like it was the first night I'd drunk with them all over again. I took a swallow, but then I wiped my mouth with the back of my hand and said, "I don't need a babysitter, Markus. You guys don't have to walk me home. I can get there on my own."

Markus took another drink. The look on his face said he needed it. He kept his voice hushed as he spoke. "I'm not sure how long I want to stay tonight myself, Stephen. So give it a little bit and then maybe we can walk each other home."

I lowered my voice, too. "Something wrong?"

He glanced over at where Devon stood, gazing silently up at the star-speckled sky, flask in his hand. "Meet me tomorrow at the library. There's something you need to see."

chapter 11

The library was just as empty as it had been the day before, but that didn't seem to bother Ms. Rose, who greeted me with a smile from behind her desk. In her hands was a well-read copy of *Flowers in the Attic* by V. C. Andrews. Sitting on the desk was a vase full of fresh wildflowers. "Hello, Stephen. What brings you in today? Let me guess. The basement?"

I offered her a smile and glanced around the room, once again cursing my lack of a cell phone. "Have you seen Markus? He told me to meet him here."

She slid a bookmark into her book and set it beside the vase. "Not yet. But I'm sure he'll be along soon."

"Guess I'll head downstairs to wait. There's more than enough in the stacks to keep me occupied."

Ms. Rose wrinkled her nose, her cheeks flushing some in embarrassment. "The dust doesn't bother you? I've been meaning to clean up that area."

I shrugged. "Dust doesn't bug me. Spiders, on the other hand . . ."

"Did you find anything to catch your interest down there?" She moved from behind the desk and picked up a big stack of books. As she struggled to carry it to one of the shelves, I moved forward and took it from her.

"Quite a bit, actually. This town has an interesting history." The stack was heavy, but getting lighter quickly as she took books from the top and placed them on the shelves. I had never figured out the Dewey decimal system, but she had it down pat. One of a librarian's many superpowers, I supposed.

As she picked up a book called *Lost Souls* by Poppy Z. Brite, she said, "I imagine you found the story about William Spencer pretty intriguing. Most people do when they start reading up on Spencer's history."

I shrugged. "You mean about him murdering his daughter? I only know what was reported in the newspapers downstairs. Anything more I should know?"

She stepped up on a small stool and stretched to put a

book away on the top shelf. The stool wobbled some, but she didn't seem to notice. Maybe super librarians could resist the pull of gravity, too. "Only if you're into gossip and mysteries." She chuckled. "It's a bit morbid, but the craziest part of the story is that he didn't just kill his daughter. People say he *sacrificed* her."

My heart beat solidly in my chest before quieting in horror. "Sacrificed? The paper said he strangled her. Or that somebody did."

"Well, now, I don't know all the details. But supposedly, after the girl died, a period of great prosperity fell on Spencer." She glanced my way, and with a wink, said, "I guess the Winged Ones were appeased, eh?"

"The Winged Ones?" I tried to act as if I'd never heard the term—as if the Winged Ones meant nothing to me—but the words came out in a gasp.

"Oh, surely you've heard that old folktale by now. Haven't you?" She peered over her shoulder at me. One of her eyebrows was raised, as if she was truly surprised that I might not know about them. As if it had been on the town's website, right next to the euchre tournament.

I chewed my bottom lip for a moment. "I might have heard something or other."

She plucked another book from the top of the pile in my arms and looked at its spine. As she put it on the top shelf, she said, "Well, they say when the Winged Ones are unhappy, they bring about bad times in Spencer until given a sacrifice."

"Who are 'they,' exactly?" Images flipped through my mind like frames of an 8mm film. The hostess at Lakehouse Grill. The old men at Tom's Hardware. The dollah-fiddy guy. Lane. Devon.

Ms. Rose lifted one shoulder in a casual shrug and dropped it just as quickly. "People around town. Small-town chatter. You know."

She stepped down from the stool and moved up the aisle again, putting a book on Abraham Lincoln on a shelf to the left and a DVD called *The Secret Life of Ferns* on a shelf to the right. I took a breath and decided to ask her the question that was stewing in my brain. Deep down, I knew the answer already. I just wanted to hear *her* answer. If someone else said it, maybe it wouldn't feel so much like I was losing my mind. "Does that mean we are . . . I mean, does that mean that *Spencer* is going through a bad time right now?"

She shook her head and grabbed a dictionary from the now much-smaller pile in my hands. As she set it on a shelf, she said, "Oh, no, not at all, Stephen. This is all just something that some folks *used* to believe and current residents use as a figure of speech or a scary story now and again. It's not like it's anything to worry about."

"Of course not. That would be crazy." It would be crazy. It would be completely nuts. So why wouldn't the tiny hairs on the back of my neck lay down again? "But I mean . . . the people who *did* believe it. How did they think the sacrifice worked, exactly?"

Ms. Rose frowned.

"I couldn't tell you. I was born in Chicago, and only came here three years ago. But it's just one of those things. Urban legends. Or in this case, it would be rural legend, I suppose." As she took the last two books from my hands, she smiled and sighed. "Anyway, I'm glad you're enjoying yourself down there. I don't get a lot of regular patrons, so it's nice to see that Markus is bringing me more."

As if on cue, the front door opened and Markus appeared, framed by the afternoon sun. He saw me and nodded. "Hey. Sorry I'm late. Had a last-minute doctor's appointment."

I couldn't help but notice the fresh cast on the arm he'd been nursing last night. "No problem, man. I hope your arm's okay. You said there was something I needed to see . . . ?"

"Yeah." He glanced at Ms. Rose before meeting my eyes with a strange glint in his. "Just thought you might wanna dig through the stacks some more. That's all."

"Well, after what Ms. Rose was just telling me, I definitely do."

I smiled at her, still trying to act like this was all a fun little project and Markus and I were just doing some research. But the truth was, I was seriously starting to question the sanity of the town I'd moved to.

An hour or so later, my leg was starting to tingle with numbness from the way I was lying with it flung over the side of the wingback chair, but I wasn't about to move—I was too immersed in yet another article I'd found in an old copy of the *Spencer Gazette* that mentioned the Winged Ones. It was the thirteenth such mention I'd found since Markus and I had come down here, and I was barely a third of the way through the pile beside the chair. I was starting to see where Devon had gotten his crazy ideas. It seemed plenty of people who'd called Spencer home over the years had either believed in the monstrous beasts or at least wondered if they actually existed. And I couldn't blame them. Spencer's history was dripping with blood—enough to ebb and flow through each period of so-called "bad times," which seemed to pop up every few years around here.

Markus's palm smacked my leg lightly. I growled and jerked away, shaking the numbness from my limb. "What?"

"We need to talk."

I sat up and placed the newspaper I'd been reading in the new pile I'd started, featuring anything and everything to do with tragedies that might be linked to the Winged Ones. "Oh, you're ready to talk now? About what?"

He shrugged his words into being. "I'm sure we can think of something to discuss. Can't we?"

I reached for the next paper in the pile. For my own sanity, I needed to keep the conversation light.

Markus knelt beside my chair, his eyes on me, his voice low. "How long have we been down here, Stephen? An hour?"

I sat the paper on my lap, giving him my full attention. "I guess, yeah. Why?"

"Found anything interesting in that time? I mean . . . anything that makes you really look closely at the people you surround yourself with?" He sounded almost like a teacher who's frustrated with a particularly hardheaded student. Markus had piled the papers next to the chair in an effort to educate me. And now he was trying to tell me something. Something about the boys. Something about Devon. I opened my mouth to speak and Markus looked around the room, as if someone might be standing in the shadows, listening. Then he rifled through the stack of newspapers beside me and pulled one paper out. As he handed it to me, we held eye contact. He shook his head. "Don't tell me what you're thinking after you read this. Don't tell anyone."

The newspaper was dated July 6 of last year. At the top of the front page, in big bold letters, was the headline of an article that made my throat dry instantly. LOCAL SHERIFF BURNED ALIVE.

It didn't take much reading for me to realize that the sheriff the reporter was talking about had been Devon and Cara's dad, and that he had died in a pretty horrific way. Officer Bradley had apparently discovered the sheriff's body floating in the reservoir, his hands bound, his skin charred, and large chunks of his flesh torn away. The autopsy had revealed that he'd been dead before he ever hit the water. Blood loss had been the apparent cause. The article went on to say that a local homeless man had been arrested and charged with murder, but the man insisted that he'd had nothing to do with the death of the sheriff.

It was horrible, and it made my stomach turn just thinking about it.

Once I'd finished reading, I sat the paper on my lap and looked pointedly at Markus. He said, "Don't say anything. Don't tell anyone I showed it to you. Just . . . just think about it. Okay?"

My jaw tightened. "I'm not a fan of secrets. Speaking of which, what happened to your arm?"

"I fell." The excuse left his lips as easy as breathing. But I didn't buy it.

"I'm not a fan of lies, either. Did Devon have anything to do with it?"

Markus grew quiet. When he spoke, he kept glancing at the bottom of the staircase, like someone might be listening. "If I told you that he did, what difference would it make? What would you do? Tell your dad? Tell the cops? If he broke my arm, he did it for a reason. If he broke my arm, it was because I did something I shouldn't have done."

"If he broke your arm, why would you stay friends with him? Are you that afraid of him?"

The room was cool, but nevertheless Markus wiped beads of sweat from his forehead with the back of his hand. His eyes fell on the stack of newspapers beside me. "Do you ever wish you'd never come to Spencer, Stephen?"

"Every damn day. But don't change the subject." I hesitated before asking the question that was hanging in the air between us, and when I finally did, my words came in a whisper. "Now tell me the truth. Did Devon break your arm?"

A scream broke off our conversation and both of us scrambled up the stairs and bolted out the library's front door. Standing directly outside was Ms. Rose, her hands cupped over her mouth, tears wetting her cheeks. She was staring across the street at the movie theater. The building's roof was entirely engulfed in flames, and smoke poured out of every window. The town cops were keeping gawkers back from the fire with outspread arms and cautionary words, but there was no fire truck in sight. The old men from the gas station were manning several garden hoses, doing their best to soak the adjoining wall of the next building so the fire wouldn't take out the whole town. I could hear sirens in the distance, but they were still pretty far away.

My memories flitted back to the night that I'd met Devon, the night we'd all broken into the theater. Memories, gone in a flicker of flame.

A small group of people had gathered by Ms. Rose to get a look at the fire. A man to her left said, "What happened?"

Someone else, a man with a deep, bellowing voice, responded, "It was the damnedest thing. Nobody was inside. She was all locked up, and this explosion just knocked the front door right off. Damn thing flew twenty feet and flames shot out from the building."

The first man whistled in amazement. "Think it was arson?"

"Cops don't think so. But it's a real mystery how else it could have started. Mighta been an electrical fire. Power to the whole building's been touch and go since Bert ran into that pole with his car."

Flames continued to spread over the outside of the building. The smoke was thick and black. If fire trucks didn't hurry, the building next to the theater was going to burn as well.

"Ain't that the damnedest thing?" A woman dressed in blue sweatpants, an orange tank top, and pink flip-flops stepped forward, her gaze glassy.

"Freak accident. Dat's what it is." I couldn't see him from where I was standing, but instantly I recognized the dollah-fiddy guy's voice.

Horrible, acrid smoke smell filled my nostrils, and I had to struggle not to gag. I covered my mouth and nose with my hand and looked around. It seemed that all of Spencer had come out to witness the blaze.

Standing apart from the crowd, his head tilted at the scene with an air of curiosity, was Devon. Markus and I hurried over, but we weren't the first to reach him. An older woman in bare feet and a blue, flowered muumuu stopped right in front of him, the expression on her face one of anguish. "You can stop this, you know. You can stop it all. You can end this."

Devon glanced over at Markus and me before returning his gaze to the fire. He didn't once look at the woman, so it was hard to tell if he was engaging her when he said, "I know."

"So do it already!" She threw her hands over her eyes, sobbing. Another woman put an arm around her and drew her back into the crowd. As they departed, Devon pulled out a pack of clove cigarettes and popped one into his mouth.

He muttered, "I'm workin' on it."

"Working on what?" I asked uneasily. I wasn't sure if Devon had meant for me to hear him or not. I wasn't sure I wanted to know the answer either way.

But Devon ignored my question. He turned to us with a wicked grin on his face.

"Anybody got any marshmallows?"

chapter 12

Water ran down my face, so hot that it burned my skin, but I continued to stand in the shower and let it wash over me and down the drain, hoping it would take my hangover with it.

After the fire yesterday, Devon had insisted on hanging out in the Playground, even though I wasn't exactly in the mood. The sight of the building burning had set me on edge. The look in Devon's eyes had set me on edge even more. But in the end, I'd decided it was probably safer if I kept Devon in my sights for the time being, so I went along and drank, just enough so that Devon wouldn't know I was onto him.

I found my dad right where I expected to find him,

sitting at the kitchen table, his hands folded in front of him. Steam rose from his favorite coffee mug—a black one that read *Goonies Never Say Die*. Beside it sat a paper plate with a small smear of butter and some toast crumbs. Mercifully, my grandmother was nowhere in sight. Probably out with her garden club or whatever else she did for fun.

Dad looked up at me, and right away he could see that I wanted to talk. He pushed the chair opposite him away from the table with his foot, inviting me to take a seat.

"Something on your mind, son?"

"Actually, yeah," I said.

I sat down at the table, realizing I hadn't quite figured out how to ask what I was wondering.

"It's about Mom."

He sucked in a breath and leaned forward in his chair.

"Well, I guess this has been a long time coming. I'm sorry the other night . . . well, I'm sorry your grandmother talked to you first."

I shrugged. "I'm just glad she turned out to be lying. I'd never forgive myself if I was halfway across the country when Mom died alone."

Dad winced. And okay, maybe I was being a little more harsh than I needed to—but only a little.

"She's okay, you know. I just spoke to the physician in charge this morning, in fact. They're trying a new medication. It has her pretty tired most of the time, but she's not ranting for the moment, so that's good."

"I guess *good* is a relative term," I said. "But anyway, that wasn't my question."

"What was your question?"

I took a deep breath. "How did you know it was time to lock Mom away? I mean, how did you know when she had crossed the line and become dangerous?"

Dad's eyes widened. I could see him trying to decide whether I was still just being a smart-ass and trying to make him suffer, or whether I was asking a serious question. Something in my eyes must have told him how serious I really was.

"Did I ever tell you how we met, your mother and I?" He ran a finger along the lip of his coffee mug as he spoke. I didn't nod or shake my head or anything, just watched him mindlessly touching his mug. He did a lot of things mindlessly, if you asked me. "There were reasons that I left Spencer straight out of high school. I never felt like I belonged here, or that anyone here understood me. Besides that, my dad ran out on me when I was six and my relationship with my mother was always . . . terse."

Terse. That was a good one. I was pretty sure that old bat idled at terse.

"It was like we were two bitter strangers residing under

the same roof, longing to be free of each other. So I worked hard, got good-enough grades to earn a scholarship to the University of Colorado, and never looked back. Second semester of my freshman year, I met the woman who would one day become your mom." He smiled, and it felt like a blast from the past. I hadn't seen my dad smile even once in the year since my mom got sick. Not a real smile, anyway. Not a smile that wasn't put on just to encourage me to smile, too. "She was beautiful. You know, the first time we met, she slapped me."

I snorted. "Go, Mom."

"Indeed." His smile broadened briefly, before reality caved in on it and shut out the happy light in his eyes. "I had it coming. But that's another story. For another time."

"Or never might be good, too." A small laugh escaped him when I said that.

"Everything was great for a while. Perfect, you might say. Well . . . maybe not perfect. What relationship is? But things were very good for a very long time between us. We were happy—happier than most couples, that's for certain. We got married the week after graduation, and four years later, had you. I didn't think life could get any better."

"I miss her." The words left my lips so easily. They sent an ache through me—the kind that can only come from a loss that deep.

"I know." Dad's eyes were bright with tears. He glanced down briefly at his hands before speaking again. "One night, about a year ago, your mother came home with this strange, wild look in her eyes, talking about another dimension that she had visited. Another world. Can you believe it? I thought she was kidding at first. Then I thought maybe she was on drugs. She kept going on about monsters with giant wings. And she was so unreachable. It was like I wasn't even in the room with her."

I shook my head. I remembered the night in question, of course. I'd been hanging out with a group of people I didn't really like all that much, and I'd come home to an empty house and a different life. But I didn't want to know this part—didn't want to hear what it had felt like to be my dad in that situation. Only, something in me thought that I needed to.

"I can't tell you how frightening that feeling is, Stephen, to not be able to connect with the person you've loved and lived with for over two decades—to not recognize the person who knows you better than you know yourself. It's terrifying." His bottom lip quivered, his eyes shimmering, and for a moment, I almost felt sorry for him. Almost. "I'd told her about Spencer and the ridiculous myth of the Winged Ones. When her mind broke, she must have clung to that image. Her brain twisted my stories into her perceived reality. For a long time, I blamed myself for her condition. I don't anymore. But I did."

Part of me thought he should. But another part of me told that part to shut the hell up.

"Right after she changed so dramatically, I took her to see a psychiatrist—I'm sure you remember. But Stephen, it was already too late. You know I tried everything to help her, and to keep her at home. All those medications, all that counseling. It amounted to little, if anything. The doctors even resorted to shock therapy for a brief, desperate time. But nothing worked. She'd be lucid for a few hours at a time, but then she'd go right back to raving." A look of shame crossed his eyes, and I was glad to see it. They had done shock therapy on her? And Mom was the crazy one? He seemed to steady himself emotionally with a few deep breaths before speaking again.

"So, to answer your question, I'm not the one who decided she was dangerous. But it was the opinion of the psychiatrists—"

"Oh, Dad, take *some* responsibility."

"Excuse me?"

"Next you're going to tell me the psychiatrists are the ones who said we should move to Spencer. That they're the ones who said if you just got rid of Mom, then poof, everything in your life would be better."

"Get *rid* of? Stephen, what in the world are you talking about? You know very well I don't plan to leave your mother alone any longer than I have to."

"If you think I'm ready to move on and leave her in the past while you work some horrible job here, you are sorely mistaken." The edges of my words burned with anger, but the anger was quickly doused by my tears. Roughly, I brushed them away with my hands.

Dad shook his head and proceeded gently. "I turned the power plant down, Stephen. You were right. No one's asking you to forget your mother."

I felt a surge of relief. That was good news at least. Still.

"Tell that to your mom." I glanced up at where my mom's teapot had been sitting.

"She just hates seeing either of us hurting, and right now, the cause of that pain is your mother, my wife."

"You're wrong. Mom's not the one hurting me." I looked pointedly at him. "You are."

He frowned, but he didn't negate what I'd said at all. "I realize that when you're seventeen a move like this can seem avoidable, needless . . . even foolish."

I snorted. "You got that right."

"But when you're in your forties and unemployed and the bills are piling up, you can recognize when your situation is desperate. We had nothing in Denver, Stephen. I'd been eating into our savings just to keep us alive, and the savings ran out. Hell, I didn't even have the cash to move us here. But I called your grandmother—and you don't know how difficult a phone call that was for me to make—and I begged her to please help us in any way she could. She offered to help us move to Spencer. And at first, I refused."

Disbelief filled me. I'd thought that the first time we had been faced with real conflict as a family, he'd tucked his tail between his legs and run home to momma. But maybe I'd been wrong about that. It had been known to happen once or twice.

"I'd spent a good portion of my life fighting to get out of Spencer. Why would I want to come back? I certainly didn't want to raise my son here. In this nowhere town, with zero opportunities for a smart, outgoing young man. People here focus on football and farming, and I wanted so much more than that for you. People here don't leave. They just grow up and mimic those who came before them. They get stuck, and I fought like hell to get unstuck. Why would I want that for you?"

Something I'd wondered myself. I would have pointed that out, but my dad was on a roll. It had taken a long time for those floodgates of communication to open, but now that they had, there was no stopping the rush of information pouring out.

"I told her no. She could keep her money. She could keep her house. She could keep it all. We wouldn't be moving to Spencer, and that was *final*." As he said the last word, he pounded his hand on the table.

"Only it wasn't final. The mortgage company sent me the foreclosure notice, and suddenly all of my friends' phones in Denver had busy signals. That's the funny thing about friends. When you're really down, people scatter like rats on a boat. When you're really down and out, family are the only people you can count on. I called my mother and pleaded for her help, which she offered up a second time—something I never thought would happen." His voice had fallen to just above a whisper. "I'm sorry if it's felt like I've dragged you here against your will, but it was against my will, too, son. I don't care for Spencer, and it's okay if you don't, either. But while we're here, you and I have to figure out a way to make it work."

We looked at each other for a good, long time without saying anything. I was the one who broke the silence, hoping to ease some—but not all—of his burden. "I am making it work. Maybe it was hard in the beginning, but I have friends now. A girlfriend, even, which is something I never had back in Denver. And up until the moment she screwed it up, I even had a halfway decent interaction with your mother the other day. So I'd say I'm making it work, Dad. As best as I can."

He gave my shoulder a squeeze. "I'm glad to hear that. And I'm sorry my mother is . . . the way she is. She's always been that way, Stephen. Since I was a kid. Bitter, pinched, mean. It's like she never wanted kids, but had one anyway."

"It must've sucked to grow up like that." I couldn't imagine what it must have been like. My dad and I might not have always had the best relationship, but I never doubted that my parents wanted a kid.

"It really did. Everything I did was wrong. Everything I said was ignored. Everything I felt was discounted."

I felt that way sometimes. Especially lately. Maybe the apple didn't really fall that far from the tree after all. "I'm sorry about your mom."

Tears poured from his eyes down his cheeks. "I'm sorry about yours."

I began to stand, not wanting anything to wreck this exchange. We hadn't shared a lot of memorable dad-and-son moments, but this one I was counting.

"Actually, Stephen, there's something I need to discuss with you, too." Drying his eyes with his hands, he pointed to my chair again, and I sat. Then he pulled a stack of papers out from under a newspaper that was sitting on the table and set it in front of me. I recognized the papers instantly. They were hand-drawn copies I'd made of the sketches in Devon's journal. No one was supposed to see them. My heart thudded in my chest.

"I found these in your room. And I want to talk about them."

"What were you doing in my room?" When I looked from the drawings to him, I could see a look in his eyes that I recognized as guilty. "Dad, those aren't—"

He tapped the papers with two fingers and looked at me pointedly. "Do you believe in these things? Do you believe in the so-called Winged Ones? I need to know, Stephen."

Mouth open, I paused, not knowing how to answer him exactly. "I . . . no. No, of course not."

But my pause had not eluded him. "Mental illness runs in the family, son. If you believe that these creatures are real, then I need to know. Your mother ranted about giant winged creatures, too. That's one of the reasons I didn't want her anywhere near here. Whatever she has . . . it might have been passed to you. But if we catch it early—"

"Dad, I'm not crazy!" I pushed my chair back and stood, slapping my palms on the table. I took in a breath and exhaled slowly, trying to remain calm. "Look, they're not my drawings, okay? They're just copies of something I found. I thought they looked interesting, I don't know. But they're not mine. They're Devon's."

"Devon?" He looked at the sketches again and ran a hand haphazardly through his hair. He was quiet for a moment, and when he spoke again, his tone was tinged with worry. "I've heard some things about that Devon kid that I don't care for."

"From who? The old men at the gas station? The guys at the hardware store?" I shook my head. "Since when do you listen to small-town gossip?"

He pushed his chair out, too, and stood. He was taller than me, but not by much. "The truth is, I don't like these friends you've been hanging out with, Stephen. Devon has trouble written all over him, and his sister can't be much better. They're exactly the kind of stuck Spencer people I didn't want you around. It has to stop. Now, son. Before you make any more poor choices." His tone said he was serious. Both serious and incredibly out of touch with reality. Had he *seen* Cara?

I pointed an accusing finger at him. "I'll watch my back when it comes to Devon, but you can forget about the idea of me breaking up with Cara. Because that is *not* going to happen."

"Be reasonable. There are other girls." He was speaking nonsense. There were no other girls. Not like Cara. She was smart and sarcastic. She was funny and sweet. She was open and real. And what's more, she was mine. You'd think he could respect that much of it anyway.

"Sure, there are other girls. There are other kids I could

hang out with. But what you're forgetting is that I *like* Cara. And at least Devon's more interesting than the other jerks in this town." How had the conversation gotten so twisted around? A minute ago, I'd been this close to flat out asking my dad whether he thought I should worry about Devon. But now, it felt like by attacking Devon, he was attacking me.

"Did your new friends tell you they put that Lane kid in the hospital?"

My body froze, but my heart raced. There was no way. He had to be wrong.

But I couldn't forget Markus's words the day Lane stole my wallet. *"The boys and I will take care of it."* Or Devon's that night: *"Probably better not to ask."*

Had they? Taken care of it?

As I moved for the front door, my dad threw out desperate, meaningless words. "Go to your room, Stephen!"

"Go to hell, Harold!" The door slammed behind me and I stepped outside into the midday sun. Standing there on the sidewalk was Cara, dressed in ragged military boots, red plaid skinny jeans, more bracelets than I could count, and some obscure band T-shirt, looking like a much-needed beacon in the middle of a stormy sea.

chapter 13

"What's wrong?" Cara fell into step beside me. And man, was I stepping. Fast and forward. The only direction that I had in mind was away.

Clenching my jaw even tighter, I practically growled, "Nothing."

"Liar." When I glanced over at her, I could see the smile in her eyes. But it faded when she realized this was more serious than just a bad day.

I softened, but was still fuming. Not at her. Never at her. "Everything."

"Liar." She grabbed the sleeve of my T-shirt and gave

it a tug, pleading with me to stop walking. We'd only made it a block from my grandmother's house, and so far my dad hadn't bothered coming after me. Cara tugged my sleeve again, getting my attention. Her eyes were so big and wondering. I wished that I could just spill my guts and tell her everything at that moment, but I couldn't risk hurting her like that. *Oh, Cara, my dad says you and your brother are trash. No big.*

A spark seemed to ignite in her mind and she laced her fingers with mine, pulling me down the street after her. "Come on. I know where we're going."

Hand in hand, we kept making our way down Water Street until we came to Second, where Cara veered us right and led me all the way to the end. We passed an older home. As we walked by, Cara pointed to it and said, "That used to be the funeral home years and years ago, but then they built a new one over on First Street. So now it's just a house. The weird thing is that the crematorium is still in the basement of this one."

It was hard to imagine the small brick Craftsman bungalow as a funeral parlor, but then again, I hadn't exactly spent much time in small towns . . . or their funeral homes. On the front porch sat a rusty tricycle that had once been painted red. Its presence made everything that Cara was saying all the more creepy. "Really? Don't they have to take them out when they're no longer in use? Isn't there a law or something? It just doesn't seem sanitary to have living people residing where corpses have been burned up. Y'know?"

She shrugged as we moved past the house and toward the end of the street. Beyond the crumbling pavement, there were trees, but nothing else. I had no idea where she was taking me. "I don't know if there's a law or whatever. I just know it's there because I've seen it. A girl I used to hang out with in elementary school lives there. We used to dare each other to go down into the basement at night and touch the oven door."

My mind whispered, *Patty cake, patty cake, baker's man*, but I wasn't certain why.

When I tried to imagine little elementary-aged Cara, with long hair in pigtails tied with ribbons, the muscles in my shoulders relaxed a little. I pictured her running back up the creaky basement stairs, squealing in fear and laughter. It was an image of pure joy, a thing of beauty, and I wondered if she ever laughed so freely now as when she'd been a little girl. Money said she didn't laugh a lot anymore at all. Not since she lost her dad in such a terrible way. Maybe before that even. A cloud hung around Cara at all times, even when she was smiling.

"Did you do it?"

"I only managed to touch it once. The rest of the times I

was too scared. I used to have these nightmares about a half-burned man reaching out and grabbing me. But at least I was braver than Brandy. She never even made it down the basement steps." Cara straightened her shoulders in pride and I made a considerable effort not to chuckle. It was such a funny thing to take pride in—that she'd once touched a cremation oven and run away from the boogeyman inside as fast as she could when her friend had not—but who was I to judge whether something was prideworthy? She'd been brave. Braver than her friend. *Patty cake, patty cake, baker's man.*

We reached the end of the pavement and I stopped at the beat-up road sign that read *Dead End*. From the time I was four until I turned eight years old, I was terrified of dead ends. I'd somehow convinced myself that whenever you saw those signs they were warnings. Of the horrors that awaited you at the end of those roads, those streets. Of monsters. But there were no monsters here. Just me and Cara.

"You and Brandy don't hang out anymore?"

"Nope. That was a long time ago. Back before this town had made up its mind about me, and before the half-burned man in my dreams became my dad." She grabbed a low-hanging branch and pulled it out of the way. As I moved past her, she raised an eyebrow at me. "What do you think? Has Spencer made up its mind about you yet?"

When I stepped through the brush, I saw that we were

standing in a clearing. Sunlight filtered through the surrounding trees, and a hush fell all around us. There was no way you could tell that we were standing mere feet outside of a town. It was quiet. It was exactly what I needed.

I shrugged in response to her question, thinking about my grandmother, about the old man from the corner shop, about Lane and his friends. "I think so."

She led me across the clearing and through another grouping of trees, until we came to an open field. We stopped and she met my eyes. "What are you gonna do about it?"

I shrugged again. "Well, if my dad doesn't get a job soon, the plan is to get through high school and get out of here, I guess."

"You'd leave?" She sat crisscross applesauce and looked up at me, her eyes filled with utter surprise. I felt guilty, but what else was I supposed to say? I couldn't lie to her. I wouldn't.

Shrugging, I tried to keep my tone casual, even though I felt in some small way like I was betraying her with every word I spoke. "Well, yeah. I want to go back to Denver. Maybe get into the University of Colorado, I don't know. I don't want to get stuck in Spencer forever. Don't you want to get out, go somewhere else?"

"Of course I do." She pulled her Tarot cards from her back pocket and shuffled them.

As she laid three cards faceup in front of her, I asked, "What are you doing?"

"Baking cookies. What does it look like? I'm reading my fortune." Her tone was snippy, which, okay, I guess was partly my fault. The way her forehead wrinkled as she looked over the cards suggested she wasn't pleased with whatever it was that she saw.

"Something wrong?" I knelt in front of her in the grass. The sun warmed my shoulders.

"I was hoping that would be the Chariot." She tapped the card on the right, the one in her future position. The corners of her pretty mouth were pulled down in a frown. "The Chariot's a card of movement. It signifies a journey."

I was interested, but probably not as interested as she needed me to be. "To where?"

"Anywhere but Spencer."

I don't know why I was surprised. Of course she wanted to leave Spencer someday. But for whatever reason, she felt like she couldn't. Maybe she didn't want to abandon her mom, the way my dad had once abandoned his mom, then later abandoned mine. I could respect that.

Reaching out, I brushed a stray hair from her eyes. She glanced at me, but refused to hold my gaze. She was mad. Not just at me. Maybe at herself. Maybe at her mom. Maybe at her life. "You could come back to Colorado with me."

"Yeah. Sure I could."

I gently lifted her chin with my hand until she was looking into my eyes at last. "You can do anything you want to do, Cara."

She turned her head away, but I could see the threat of tears in her eyes. "Right. Sure I can."

A breeze arrived without warning, pressing the long grass all around us down again and again, making it look like ripples in a lake. I sighed, but the breeze picked up and swallowed the sound. To my surprise, the cards remained where they were on the ground, undisturbed. I nodded to the ones she'd laid out. "So what's it all mean?"

Cara closed her eyes, letting the wind brush back her hair and dry her cheeks. When she opened her eyes again, she seemed a little more at peace. She pointed to the cards and said, "In my past is the Sun. It's pretty much the happiest card you can get. It stands for relationships, friendship, joy. It might be referring to my childhood. Before everything went to hell. In my present is the Moon. . . ."

She furrowed her brow and stared at the cards, as if something there had disturbed her further. I waited a moment before speaking. "And?"

Cara shook her head. "Why don't I just read yours now? You can't possibly be all that interested in my future."

It was a dig about my plans to leave Spencer, but I shook

it off. "I'm kinda hoping to be a part of it. So could you keep reading, please?"

There was a moment when time slowed, when all we did was look at each other, the threat of my leaving hanging between us. Then Cara gathered the cards into a pile and said, "In my future is the World. It stands for triumph."

I shrugged. "That sounds good."

"I still wish it had been the Chariot." She dropped the deck in front of me. "Shuffle the cards and cut them as many times as you want."

The tension between us was uneasy and strange, and I found myself fighting just to get through it, like walking over marshland. I wanted to apologize, but at the same time, I wanted her to recognize that I had my own problems to deal with. And so what if I didn't plan to spend my entire life stuck in a nowhere town, filled with no one and nothing to do. It was my life, wasn't it?

I took the cards from her and shuffled them quickly and cut them before handing them back, biting my tongue. She laid out three cards. Past, present, future. Left to right they looked like a guy running along and not looking where he was going, a dude hanging upside down by his ankle, and a creepy lone man cowering from an unseen force. My life, just looking at the pictures, was pretty grim. I let out a sigh, and Cara pointed to the first card. "In your past, you have the

Fool. This card means innocence, naivety, and spontaneity. Maybe you didn't know something, but you moved forward anyway in ignorant bliss."

The conversation I'd just had with my dad refused to leave my mind. I shook my head. "Bliss. Yeah. That doesn't sound like what I'm going through."

"That card shows more ignorance than bliss. Besides, it's in your past." She tapped the card next to it. A ladybug crawled from the grass onto the card before taking a journey across the second guy's head. "*This* is in your present. The Hanged Man. It signifies devotion to a worthwhile cause, temporary suspension of progress. It's all about sacrificing one thing to obtain another."

Suspension of progress? Now that sounded exactly like my present state. Was the card saying I was stuck? Because I sure as hell felt stuck. Stuck in Spencer. Stuck with my grandmother. Stuck under my dad's control until I hit eighteen. Devotion to a worthwhile cause could've been my relationship with Cara. But what was I sacrificing in order to obtain something else? Was I sacrificing my dad's approval to be with Cara? Made sense.

I eyed the third card, the dude cowering from something not shown in the picture. I didn't know why, but seeing the card sent a small shiver up my spine. I wasn't about to tell Cara that. I nodded toward it as casually as I could manage. "What about that one?"

She ran the fingertips of her right hand over the last card, a small crease forming on her brow. "The Hermit . . ."

She paused, looking troubled. I shuffled a nervous glance between her and the card.

". . . is a card of caution. It points to a need to reach into one's inner resources, and a time to stand back and reflect upon circumstances."

So basically, the creepy guy thought I needed to look inside myself for the answers to my problems . . . or some such crock. Who did he think he was, cardboard Yoda? I snorted in derision and rolled my eyes at Cara. "Very helpful. Do you really, actually believe in this stuff?"

As lighthearted as I'd meant it, my question clearly hurt her feelings. "If I didn't believe in Tarot, would I bother doing it?"

Groaning, I stood, brushing grass from my legs. "Lots of people do things on a regular basis that they don't believe in, Cara."

"Such as?" She started picking up the cards quickly, angrily, and stacking them together in her hand.

"Nothing. Never mind. I'm sorry. I just can't do this today. Tomorrow, okay?" I bent down and took her chin in my hand, tilting her face up to mine. I was sorry I was being such a dick to her. It wasn't her fault I was feeling sorry for myself. It wasn't her fault that my family was so screwed up. But I was taking it out on her just the same. "Tomorrow. When I can be good to you."

She closed her eyes briefly, and when she opened them, they were sad. She said, "What's the point in being together if we can't be together through good and bad?"

She'd made a very wise point. But I had to leave, had to get away from her. I was hurting and in the mood to make someone else hurt, too. But not Cara. Anybody but Cara.

Shaking my head, I moved back toward the trees. "I just . . . can't."

"Stephen . . ."

I didn't look back at her as I disappeared the way we'd come. I only held up a hand in a reluctant wave and made us both a weak promise that neither of us could trust. "Tomorrow."

She didn't follow me—something that I was both grateful for and disappointed in. I'd known girls who chased guys, promising them anything just to get the guys to do whatever it was that the girls wanted them to do. I couldn't respect girls like that, which was one of the reasons I found Cara so irresistible. She was her own person. Smart, strong, independent, but loyal at the same time. I loved that she didn't call out after me. But I hated it at the same time. Because the truth was, I wanted her to stop me. I was so torn, it was making my head ache.

No sooner had I pushed through the second line of trees and stepped onto the pavement than I noticed Devon and Markus heading north on a cross street. Jogging, I caught up with them relatively quickly. "Hey. What's going on?"

They exchanged glances before Markus shrugged. "Not much. Just getting a few things in order before we head to the Playground tonight."

Devon shot him a look that screamed *shut up*. It brought an immediate question to my lips. "Anything I can help with?"

Devon nodded for Markus to keep going on without him. Markus continued up the street, joining Nick and Thorne, who were standing outside a liquor store that looked like it doubled as a Laundromat. When Devon turned back to me, his eyes took on a steely gaze, as if I were causing a problem. "You're not invited tonight, Stephen."

I had no idea where this was coming from. Was he embarrassed after telling me they believed in stories about giant, winged monsters? Because all sorts of people believed in all sorts of things, as Cara had reminded me. I didn't care.

I said, "Come on. Seriously? I need to get outta the house. My dad—"

"Stephen." Devon's eyes went cold. "Not tonight."

"Why?"

"Because I said." He looked over his shoulder and I followed his line of sight. A man who I'd guess was homeless by the looks of him had stepped out of the liquor store and was engaging in conversation with Markus and the others. Even from this distance, I could see the ugly hat on the man's head. It looked like something a fisherman would wear, only instead of various hooks and bobbers, it featured ugly patches of several different colors.

After a moment, Markus waved to Devon. Devon nodded and turned back to me. "Look, tonight's about me and the boys. Go home, sleep off what's left of that hangover, and tomorrow everything will be right as rain."

"Tomorrow?" My stomach clenched. He was making me the same promise I'd made to his sister not ten minutes before. Whether or not either promise was an empty one remained to be seen.

"Yeah. You have my word on that." He slapped me on the back and continued his trek toward the liquor store and the rest of the boys.

I called after him, "Who's the guy?"

He didn't turn back to me—Devon was finished with this conversation. But as a small token of our friendship, he shouted his best advice. "Trust me, Stephen. The fewer questions you ask, the better off you'll be."

"Devon, have you seen Lane?" I called, but he didn't answer or turn around at all. Maybe he didn't hear me. I hoped he just didn't hear me, and wasn't avoiding the question altogether. I really wanted to believe that Devon was a boy that Spencer had the wrong idea about. That even if he was a little off, he was no more dangerous than the rest of us. But I had a feeling he knew exactly where Lane was. And where Lane was just might be in a hospital bed two towns over.

I hoped that man was just buying their liquor.

Later that night, after I'd walked everywhere I could think of that wasn't anywhere near our block, I snuck back inside my grandmother's house and stowed away in my room, successfully dodging my dad on the way. Moonlight drifted into my room, painting everything a pale blue. It was a full moon tonight, and surprisingly cool. A voice in the back of my head kept whispering, but I put on some music and tried not to listen to it. Even so, the voice came through loud and clear.

As any Hollywood movie could tell you, a lot of rituals were tied to the full moon. For everyone from ancient Mayans to voodoo conjurers to modern-day witches, full moons were supposed to be the nights for performing all sorts of crazy shit . . . including sacrifices.

Devon's voice echoed through my mind. *"It's said that the only way to appease their fury, the only way to make the bad times go away again . . . is by offering up a human sacrifice."*

Okay, so Devon and the others believed in the existence of the Winged Ones. That seemed hard to deny after everything. But how far would they be willing to go to appease the monsters and bring about an end to Spencer's so-called "bad times"? Would they kill a man? Maybe a homeless man who they'd encountered outside of the liquor store? If my hunch was correct, Devon may have been responsible for one death already.

Just how far were the boys willing to go for a belief?

How far was I willing to go for mine?

chapter 14

The next morning, I rose early—mostly because I'd barely slept the night before. How could I sleep when my brain absolutely refused to shut up, and my imagination insisted on dredging up horrific images of Devon and the guys taking the life of some helpless guy, just to slake the bloodthirst of imaginary flying monsters?

So instead, I tossed and turned and tried as hard as I could to make sense of it all. And try as I might to be logical and sensible, my thoughts kept going back to Devon's journal. I might not believe in the Winged Ones, but the boys clearly did. And belief was a funny thing. It made people do things that theories and ideas couldn't. Beliefs made people associate with certain people or not. Beliefs made people give money to certain causes or avoid them altogether. Beliefs made people sacrifice, be it luxuries or lives. Ideas could be changed. Theories could be modified. But beliefs were hard-core. They were solid. They were something that the believers took very, very seriously. And the notion that Devon, Markus, and the others believed in something I expected to encounter only on late-night TV scared the hell out of me. Not because the monsters might exist—really. But because my friends might be on their side.

The sun had barely come up when I stepped out the front door, and as I passed Devon and Cara's house, I felt like I was walking through a ghost town. No lights were on in any of the windows I passed. No people were moving about on the streets. No human sounds were in the air. It was just me and my footfalls moving through the town of Spencer before anyone else was awake.

I had to visit the Playground—had to know if there was any real, solid reason to suspect Devon and the boys of wrongdoing. But I had to do it when I could be relatively certain that no one else would be around.

For once, I felt safer during the day.

So I moved as silently as I could and hoped that no one would see me. As I passed a house on the far end of town, only about a block from the cemetery, I thought I saw a curtain move, and my heart jumped into my throat. It was paranoia, I was sure. No one was watching me. The boys weren't really killing people in order to save their hometown from ancient beings. The entire town wasn't somehow in on it. I was being ridiculous. My imagination was on overdrive—something not out of the realm of possibility.

But . . . if I had dreamed up the entire idea, then why was my heart rattling inside my chest as I reached the Playground and passed William Spencer's headstone? Why did I have a gut feeling that said I should be extremely careful in my search, so that I would have proof to show the police? Because deep down, I was already convinced that Devon, Markus, and the others had done something truly horrible.

And even if I was wrong about the rest of the boys, I didn't have to dig very deep to find my belief that Devon would resort to something like that. Devon had a touch of Martha in him, for sure. And, more dangerous still, the kid had nothing to lose.

A thin layer of fog covered the cemetery, snaking between the tall tombstones. The ground looked marshy at first glance, but that observation proved wrong when I crossed the grass between the graves. I looked around every stone I saw, hoping for either irrefutable evidence to prove my terrible theories or else a lack of evidence to prove my friends' innocence. I left the tallest tombstone for last. That was Devon's stone—the one he liked to perch on top of. If there was evidence of ritual sacrifice anywhere, it would be there.

Ritual sacrifice? Really? Was that what I was looking to prove? The idea sounded so insane, even though it seemed entirely plausible. I needed evidence, because without it, who was going to believe me? Without it . . . how could I be sure I even believed myself?

The ground around Saint Devon's perch was bare—nothing but dirt and rocks and dying grass. Sighing heavily, I turned toward where the road dead-ended, where Devon had nearly killed me that first night with the group. The thought entered my mind jumbled, but quickly that jumble turned into what seemed like an obvious question. What if Devon had pushed the homeless man off the cliff? He wouldn't even need the help of the guys to do that.

Gravel crunched under my shoes as I approached the cliff. Crouching, I looked over the edge, but saw nothing. No remnants of the man's clothes, no evidence of blood or even a struggle. I began to stand again, but something caught my eye. It was small, relatively thin, and poking out from under my shoe. I moved my foot and picked it up, turning it over in my hand to examine it. Rope. The ends of it were burnt. It was probably nothing, but it might've been everything. I walked back toward town, shoving the bit of rope into my front pocket. Maybe my friends had been pulling my leg about believing in the Winged Ones. Maybe this was all part of the same joke that began the night Devon pushed me over the edge. In a way, finding inconclusive evidence was the worst thing that could have happened.

But my thoughts turned to the cast on Markus's arm, and the fear in his eyes when I'd asked him if it had been Devon's doing.

No one could possibly understand how I was feeling. But one person could make me forget about it—if only for a little while. And if I happened to see her brother in the process, well, I could confront him about what happened and kill two birds with one stone.

As quickly and quietly as I could, I made my way to Cara's front yard and tossed a discarded bottle cap at her window. The metal made a *tick* sound as it bounced off the glass, and I wasn't sure if she'd heard it or not. But then a moment later, her bedroom window opened, and she poked her head outside. Her hair was tangled and yesterday's eyeliner was smudged all around her half-asleep eyes, but I'd never seen her look so beautiful, so real. Remembering the last words I'd said to her, I whispered loudly, hoping not to wake anyone else. "It's tomorrow."

"Barely." She snorted, rolling her eyes. "What do you want?"

She was pissed, and rightfully so. Suddenly, I was sorry for not telling her about my dad and what he'd said about breaking up with her. Suddenly, I wanted to tell her everything and anything else that she wanted to know. Because she was important to me. Because she was the only thing in my life that didn't make me question who I was or what I was doing. Tilting my head slightly to the right, I smiled up at her. "To apologize for acting like a jerk. Is that okay?"

The corner of her mouth lifted in a sultry smirk. "Yeah. But it'll be better if you come inside. Just be quiet on the stairs. Don't wake up my mom."

"Or Devon."

"He didn't come home last night. Probably staying with Markus or something." Her words gave me pause, but there wasn't much more I could do about it now. Stepping up on the porch, I moved as quietly as I could, crossing the old, creaking boards and opening the door. The hinges squeaked, sending a barrage of swear words through my mind. I crept up the stairs and each step squeaked, too. It was as if the entire house were trying to do me in and prevent me from ever getting inside Cara's room again.

At the top of the stairs was a small hallway, and to the right there was an open door. Cara's room was to the left, and I was pretty certain that Martha's room was downstairs on the main level. So that had to be Devon's room. Curiosity steered me right and plain old nosiness flipped on the light.

There were no windows in Devon's room, and the room itself was only about half the size of Cara's. The far wall featured a closet, its entire door covered with posters from bands. Old bands like the Ramones and the Sex Pistols were featured right alongside the White Stripes and Florence and the Machine. A bookcase took up the rest of that wall, but few books occupied the space. Instead, Devon had an impressive collection of vinyl. A record player sat to the right of his bed instead of a nightstand. Each wall was painted a different jewel tone, but the bedding on his queen-sized mattress was all black. To the left of his bed sat a freestanding shelf, with a menagerie of weirdness. One shelf held an anatomical model of a hand—the wooden kind that artists use for drawing. It was posed with its middle finger up, flipping the bird to all who entered his domain. On the shelf below that sat six old dolls' heads—none with eyes. On the shelf below those sat a half-empty two liter of Mountain Dew and a jar filled with some viscous liquid, along with something that looked like it might have once been alive. Something else was laying on the shelf, but I couldn't quite make it out without picking it up. I took a step farther in, and headed for the shelf.

"Wanna see something cool?" Cara's voice made me jump. My heart flew into my throat and I stumbled backward before realizing that it was her. Giggling, she gave my shoulder a playful shove and nodded into the room. "He painted liquid Tide on the walls. You know, the laundry detergent. It glows under black light."

She flipped the wall switch, turning off the overhead light, and I heard her clicking something on to my left. Suddenly, the walls lit up with her brother's artistry. I stood there in shock for a moment, almost unable to breathe.

On the wall behind his bed, a pair of giant wings had been painted in broad, almost frightening brushstrokes. The wings glowed blue under the black light. But what had shaken me to my core were the words painted beneath them.

All things to Them. All lives for Them. All praise the Winged Ones.

As Cara flipped the ceiling light back on, my eyes caught the unidentified item on the bottom shelf by the bed. I didn't know why I hadn't recognized it before, but now it seemed so obvious.

It was the homeless man's hat.

Devon must have killed the man and taken his hat as a memento. Simple as that. But if Devon hadn't come home last night, when had it gotten here?

Cara hadn't noticed anything out of the ordinary, and I wasn't about to tell her she was living with two lunatics instead of just one. No, I was going to turn her brother in, and then take Cara away from this town, this place, this family. I was going to save her. The way that no one else could. The way that no one else would.

"Come on." She gave my sleeve a tug before releasing it and moving down the hall to her room. After she was out of sight, I grabbed the hat and hid it behind my back, exiting Devon's room with an awkward shuffle. On the way out, I noticed an old, beat-up baseball bat sitting beside Devon's door. Painted on it in bright red were the words *problem solver*.

Cara was already sitting on her bed when I got to her room, and immediately patted the seat next to her. Crossing the room, I felt my heart racing, but not because of the flirtatious look in her eyes or the fact that she'd just beckoned me to her bed.

Her bed. That place that she slept at night. Possibly naked.

My heart was racing because of what I was holding in my hand, and what it would mean if I gave it to the police and explained what Devon had done. It would mean Cara losing her brother. It would mean crushing her, just to save her. But I had to do it. There was no other way.

As I took a seat beside her, I carefully dropped the hat to the floor. Cara lay back on the bed, bringing me with her. She laid her head on my chest and we stayed like that, silent, for several minutes. Her cheek felt warm, even through the fabric of my shirt. I could have lain there for hours, days, months, years, forever.

It was Cara who finally broke the silence. "So about that apology . . ."

Running a hand over her silky black hair, I said, "I'm sorry. Really. I shouldn't have left like that."

Her words were hushed. "You were acting so weird, and then you just took off. Were you mad at me or something?"

"No." I swallowed hard, and tried to pry my thoughts from the hat on the floor. "Not just you. I've been avoiding everything. Things are just rough right now, y'know?"

"Don't do that again. I may not forgive you so easily next time." She flashed me a small smile and then ran her fingers over my chest. I melted a little into the mattress. "What's wrong?"

"It's . . . nothing."

"You're lying to me. Something is really bothering you, Stephen. I can see it in your eyes. Tell me." She sat up then, sudden, overwhelming concern in her eyes. "Did Devon do something?"

"No." I sat up, too, wishing so much that we could just go back to lying down together and not talk about her brother. Or murder. Or monsters that might or might not be real.

"Did I?"

"No. No, Cara. It's nothing like that." I rested on my elbows, the half-truth ready, aimed, and cocked. "Look, I'm just having a really hard time lately, with my grandmother and my dad and all. It's just stress. Promise."

She narrowed her eyes. "I'm not sure if I believe you."

I reached out with my right hand and cupped her chin in my palm. The way her makeup was smudged made her look so young, so innocent, so lost. "I'd do anything to protect you, y'know. Even if it meant hurting you."

She grabbed my hand in hers. "You're scaring me, Stephen. What's going on?"

"Nothing. I'm sorry." I pulled my hand away and lay back on the bed, wishing that she'd join me. Wishing that I could just forget about all of this and go back to thinking about her fingernails scraping slowly across the skin on her thigh. But it was too late for that. This had to be dealt with. And soon.

"About what? What are you sorry for?"

"I can't really say." I swallowed again, my throat getting drier by the second. To save her, I had to hurt her. To do the right thing, I had to betray her trust completely. I shook my head, the words soft on my tongue. "Not yet."

First, I'd try the police. I'd give them the hat and tell them everything they needed to know. I'd answer any questions they asked. I'd do whatever they wanted me to do to help prove this case. And if they didn't believe me, I'd find another way.

And if all else failed, I'd have to confront Devon myself.

chapter 15

I'd crept out of Cara's house before Martha showed up and told me that I was going to burn in hell for groping her teenage daughter—which I totally didn't do during this particular visit—but I didn't go home. Instead, I crossed town with my head down, hoping like hell I wouldn't run into any of the boys and have to face questions about where I was going and what I was doing. A strange mixture of urgency and shame filled me. For so long, I'd blamed my dad for locking my mom away, and now here I was, about to turn Cara's brother in to the police. Some friend I was.

But I wouldn't be able to sleep at night knowing that my

inaction would allow Devon to get away with what he'd done. What I was pretty positive he'd done. What I hoped he hadn't done.

I couldn't rest knowing that Devon probably suffered from the same kind of mental illness that afflicted Martha, and very much needed someone to step up and say something so that he could get the help that he needed. I cared about him, and I knew right from wrong. That was why I was doing what some might call betrayal. Because, I could see now, it was the right thing to do.

The small brick building sat in the northeast part of town, just to the right and up a block from that dollah-fiddy guy's store. Halfway there, I wondered if the police station had certain office hours, or if you could just walk in any time, like a 7-Eleven. Which brought to mind the insane image of me sipping on a twenty-two-ounce half-cherry, half-Coke Slurpee while trying to explain that my friends were in some kind of cult that worshipped giant bird monsters. And worse. It was more like they believed that if someone died, the boogeyman would go away, and all the town's problems would be solved. *Patty cake, patty cake, baker's man.*

I was still shaking my head about it when I stepped up on the landing right outside the door to the small police station. The lights were on inside, so I grabbed the handle and opened the door. As I did so, a small bell jingled over my head. It surprised me to hear it. Did all the buildings in this town have bells? And if so, why? To alert the locals that they had company? To warn them?

The two uniformed men sitting inside turned their heads toward me expectantly. Wondering which one of them might be the Officer Bradley who disliked Cara so much, I squeezed the hat in my hands and took a deep, slow breath.

The thinner of the two stood and kind of squinted his eyes at me. "You're that new kid, ain't you?"

Great. The local police already knew me. Cara's voice rang in my ears. *"Has Spencer made up its mind about you yet?"* In answer to her, and to the officer who was speaking to me, I simply said, "Yeah."

The cop nodded in return. "Yeah, your dad's ol' Betty's boy. His name's Harvey or Harry or something."

"Harold. You remember him, Ted. Went to school with us. Scrawny kid, never could catch a ball." As if demonstrating how talented he himself had been at sports, the officer threw the apple in his hand up in the air about a foot and caught it effortlessly in one hand. Beneath the jowls, I could see the former Johnny Football in him. He was that guy who'd peaked in high school, the one who everybody probably still bowed down to at Friday night JV practice. Or whenever, whatever. I didn't really know much about sports. But I could tell that he didn't seem to care much for my dad, just from the way he'd said his name.

"You're Harold's kid?" The thinner cop slapped his chubby buddy on the back and chuckled like my dad was the best bad joke he'd ever heard. "Guy was a loser if I ever saw one."

"Can we please get to why I'm here?" I must have spoken pretty loudly, because both of them stopped chuckling and looked right at me like I was some kind of criminal. But so what if I'd raised my voice? This was important. Far more important than reliving their high school glory days. "I'd like to make a report."

"So?" Johnny Football took a bite of his apple. When he spoke again, bits of it flew from his open mouth. "Make it."

I'd never made a police report before, and honestly hadn't once set foot inside a police station. But I'd learned from watching *Judge Judy* that police reports were important. I'd also learned that pissing off Judge Judy meant that she would unhinge her jaw and come after you. And possibly your children. I could tell I was nervous, because even my imagination had begun babbling. Shut up, brain.

I looked at the thinner cop, who was shuffling some papers around his desk. He might have actually been organizing them, but my money was on the fact that he was just trying to appear busy so that maybe I'd take the hint and go away. No dice. "Can I do so anonymously? I mean, without anyone finding out that it was me who came here and told you what I'm about to tell you?"

Ted dropped the papers he'd been organizing into a messy pile on the corner of his desk and snorted. "That ain't how we run things around here, sport. You tell us whatchoo gotta tell us, and we'll see that it's handled."

It was only then that I noticed the wall to the left, which was home to several pieces of paper starring wanted criminals or missing persons . . . and a painting of three enormous, feathered creatures, swooping over a small, quaint-looking town. My throat dried instantly. "What's that painting about anyway? You guys just like birds around here or what?"

Johnny Football sat forward in his seat and looked at me, half-eaten apple in his hand. As he moved, his chair groaned under his weight. "Ain't you never heard of the Winged Ones?"

"Brian." Ted shot him a warning look—one that grabbed my interest with both hands and refused to let go.

"Now, c'mon, Ted. I figure if the boy calls Spencer home now, he should know a little about her history." When Brian looked back at me, he wiped some apple juice or drool or something from his chin and said, "Local legend says that these things with giant wings have been appearing in Spencer for hundreds of years. They used to cause quite a ruckus, killed a lot of people."

None of this was news to me. "Why'd they stop?" I quipped.

"Some say people started giving them offerings. Some say people started sacrificing outsiders to the creatures to get them to calm down and leave our town alone." He stood— no longer Johnny Football, now Brian the Man in Charge in Spencer—and lowered his voice, as if we shared some twisted, dark secret. In a way, we did. "But you got nothing to worry about there, do ya, boy? You're one of Spencer's own. Daddy was born and raised in this town. You're safe as safe can be. Safe as kittens, as they say. Oh . . . but then your daddy moved. So I guess you're not safe after all."

When at last I managed to speak, it was a miracle that dust didn't come out. My throat and tongue were so dry. My words were strangled whispers. "I'd like to make my report now, please."

Ted shifted a few more papers on his desk over to one corner. "Like I said, go ahead. We're listening."

I had to force the words out. No matter what anyone might think or say. "I think that the guys I've been hanging out with might be planning to kill someone."

Brian didn't miss a beat. "Now why on earth would they do that?"

Clutching the hat in my hands, I glanced at Ted before sharing my theory—which I already had a sneaking suspicion would be useless. This was my fight. I was the only one who could stop Devon now. "I think they believe that the Winged Ones are real."

The air felt heavy. Beads of sweat started to form on my forehead. Then Brian leaned closer and said, "Don't you?"

I opened my mouth and began to speak, but it took me a moment. "I—"

"Don't everybody?" It might have been my imagination, but it sounded like Brian had raised his voice. Just enough to let me know that if I wasn't with them, I was against them.

Ted shook his head. "Shoot, Brian, you'd best be kinder to our guest here. Boy's just tryin' to make a report."

My breathing came a bit easier then, and I nodded my gratitude to him. "Thank you."

"Besides. Ain't our business if he gets gobbled up by those beasts. That being said, I'll be glad to see the bad times taken care of again. Less paperwork that way." Ted and Brian exchanged looks before bursting into laughter. I wasn't an informant after all. It turned out I was a punch line.

Brian slapped his knee repeatedly. His face was beet red.

It was my turn to raise my voice. "You don't understand. Something is happening in this town. Something real. Something dark. You have to help me. You're the local law enforcement, aren't you? You have to do something."

Their laughter stopped. From where he sat, Brian

pointed a long, mean finger at me. "We don't gotta do diddly-squat. Now mind your manners."

Ted sat on his desk and looked at me, curious. He probably thought I was crazy. Maybe I was. "Tell me, son. Do you actually believe the Winged Ones are real? Tell me true now."

"I'm trying to explain something to you." My mind began playing footage of everything that I'd seen since moving to Spencer. The feathers in the cemetery. Devon's journal. The burnt pieces of rope.

"Do you?"

Markus's cast. The burning theater. The look on Devon's face as he gazed up into the night sky. "If you would just listen to me. These guys have killed someone. I think they may kill again."

"Do you?"

The painting on Devon's bedroom wall. The hat. The hat. The hat. "I found this guy's hat in my friend's room, and if you would just go to the Playground tonight, then maybe—"

"Do you believe in them?"

"I don't know anymore!" My heart all but seized. I sucked in a breath, and as I exhaled, I noticed that my hands were shaking.

Brian's voice was hushed—the quietest it had been since I'd entered the building. "Well. Ain't that somethin'?"

"I . . . I just . . ." I looked around the room. There was no one to help me now. There was nothing more to say. "I have to go."

Without another word, I turned and got out as fast as I could. The bell jingled as I opened the door and Ted said, "Where you runnin' to, boy?"

Brian's voice chased after me as I stepped outside, completely on my own now. "Say hi to Harvey for us!"

"Harold."

"Whatever."

It was up to me. Not the cops. Not anyone else. It was up to me to stop Devon and the boys from killing again.

I needed to plan my next move, before the boys made their next move first.

chapter 16

I spent the rest of the morning inside—trying to figure out what to do about the possibility that my friend was a murderer. For once, I was glad to have a few mindless chores to keep me distracted. The world outside might be going to hell in a handbasket, but the fresh coat of paint in the kitchen was looking quite nice.

I took the recycling bin out to the end of the driveway, squinting against the brightness of the sun. When I got back to the front door, something small, white, and square caught my attention to the left. A piece of paper had been tucked carefully into the window screen of my bedroom. I wanted not to see it, but it was there, plain as day. As unavoidable as heat in summer. And without even looking, I knew what it was.

Carefully navigating the narrow passageway between shrubbery and the outer wall, I snatched the piece of paper from its place and unfolded it, revealing a note from Devon. I could tell it was from Devon, because the handwriting matched exactly what had been inside of his journal. His note was messy, almost scratched onto the page. The last four words were written boldly, as if he'd gone over them with the pen several times.

Tonight. Midnight. Playground.
We need to talk.

That we did. Because I needed answers. I needed to know if my suspicions, my fears, had any basis in reality, or if this was all just some horrible misunderstanding. I needed answers to my questions, and I needed them quickly.

I crumpled up the note and slipped it inside my front pocket.

Yes. Yes. Yes. My friends would kill me to keep their secret. They would kill me to ensure my silence. They would kill me, period. I still had no choice but to face them. Tonight.

I moved inside the front door, and with a dry throat and a furrowed brow, I picked up the house phone from its cradle on the table in the parlor. I knew the number I was dialing by heart, despite the fact that I'd never succeeded in calling it from Spencer. And I had to call. It was now or never.

When the woman on the other end answered, my heart sank into my shoes. I knew what I had to do. I knew what I had to say. I was reluctant, but determined nonetheless.

"Denver Psychiatric Hospital, inpatient call line. How may I direct your call?"

I'd made calls to the hospital regularly up until the day we'd left Denver. Dad hadn't had to nudge as often back then, back before I was feeling so bitter about the changes that had been forced into my life. It felt like such a foreign experience calling from Spencer. I was in another world, on another planet, trying desperately to reach through the cosmos and make a much needed connection with my past. "Hi. Um. I need to reach my mother, Margaret Truax. She's a patient there. My name is Stephen Truax."

The sound of typing on a computer keyboard came through the receiver. Then she answered, "Please hold. I'll patch you in to her floor."

"Stephen?" I recognized the voice on the other end as one of the nurses we'd regularly interacted with during our all-too-brief visits with my mom. Her name was Sharon, or

Sherry, or something like that. I strained my memory, but couldn't quite grasp it. She didn't wait for me to respond, only said in a chipper voice, "I've got your mom right here. Hold on."

There was a brief shuffle on the other end, and while it was happening, my eyes found the phone cradle on the table in a moment of doubt. Maybe it would be best if I didn't talk to her. Maybe some things were better left unsaid. "Hello?"

Her voice sounded so normal, so lovely and lilting. It brought a small smile to my lips. "Hi, Mom. It's Stephen."

"Oh, that's nice. It's Stephen! Everyone, it's Stephen. How are you, baby?"

Baby. She always called me baby. I could be seventy years old and the president of a Fortune 500 company, and my mother would still call me baby. This time, I didn't roll my eyes when she did it. Instead, I secretly reveled in it.

"I'm fine, Mom. Listen . . ." Gripping the phone to my ear, I said, "I need to tell you something, and I'm not sure you'll understand. But just in case something happens, I need to tell you . . . good-bye."

"Good-bye?" Her tone dropped, and sadness invaded the air. On both ends of the call.

We were both mourning my death before it even happened. I was, anyway. It was hard to say what was going through my mother's mind. But I liked to think that on some level, she understood what I was saying. One way or another, Devon and the boys would make sure I never left Spencer.

"Yeah. Look, Mom," I whispered into the receiver, not wanting anyone to overhear. "I . . . I have something to do, something really important, and I might not be able to call you again. So I wanted—"

She interrupted, her tone dark and disturbing. An alarmed tingle shot up my spine as she spoke. "You've got to fight them, Stephen. You've got to fight them and kill them. They'll never stop! They'll never—"

The nurse broke in then, sounding more than a little bit exasperated. "Hello, Stephen? Sorry about that. She's due for her medication. Would you care to leave a message for when she's feeling better?"

Monsters. My mother had been fighting monsters this entire time. And I'd thought nothing of it. Now I had to fight some monsters of my own.

I cleared my throat before responding in a hush. "Just . . . just tell her that I love her, okay?"

"Will do."

As I returned the phone to its cradle, I noticed my dad standing near the door, his arms folded in front of him, a concerned look on his face. "How much did you hear?"

He shrugged slightly. "Just the end. Was she ranting?"

"Some." Enough. It turned out she'd ranted enough.

"That happens whenever I call lately."

The center of my chest felt hollow and heavy. I could feel my eyes moistening, but fought to keep my tears at bay. "Does she . . . does she ask about me?"

He smiled, his eyes shimmering. "All the time, son. All the time."

He turned to walk out the front door, but before he could, I said, "Dad? I love you."

I knew my words had shocked him. Of course they had. I never said those things. Not since I was ten years old. Maybe even earlier. I never said I loved him. I just had always assumed he knew. But not today. Today I needed to make sure I said it and that he heard me, and that he knew I meant every word. Just in case.

"I know. I love you, too." He turned from the door and tilted his head at me in obvious concern. "Everything okay?"

Shaking my head, I forced a chuckle. "Yeah. Just feeling a little nostalgic, I guess."

He nodded, but it didn't really look like he believed me. "Hey. About our conversation yesterday. That was just me trying to control the uncontrollable, okay? I know you'll make good decisions moving forward. I was just feeling a little left out of your life, that's all. Are we good?"

"Yeah. We're good." And we were. That part, at least,

wasn't a lie. Dad and I were good. At last.

"I've gotta run some errands for your grandmother now, but maybe tonight we can go back to the diner for a nice dinner, just the two of us. I can tell you all about the exciting news I just got."

I raised my eyebrow in a question.

"Well, okay, I'll spoil it now—I got a job offer! It's a little bit of a pay cut compared to my last job, but it's in Saint Louis, right next to a great mental health center. So at least we'd be getting out of Spencer." A chuckle escaped him as he grabbed the doorknob and pulled. A strangely cool breeze wafted into the house, billowing the parlor curtains. "That means we can move your mom there, closer to us. It's not perfect, but at least we'll be together."

I put on my best fake smile, hoping it would be enough to convince him to leave. "That's great, Dad. All of it."

He raised a questioning eyebrow, and I thought he might never go. "Sure you're okay?"

I donned my best lying smile. "Couldn't be better."

After he walked out the door, I crossed through the kitchen on my way to my room. Midnight would be here before I knew it and I wanted to have time to gather my thoughts and formulate my plan before it got here. Sitting at the kitchen table was my grandmother, a ball of red yarn in front of her, a metal hook in her right hand. She was in the middle of creating something that looked a lot like a scarf. I almost walked by without saying a word, but at the last moment, I stopped and stood by the table, watching her hands, wishing we had a very different relationship than we did. It might have been nice to have a grandmother. Not this one. But some other grandmother. "Have you been knitting long?"

She didn't look at me, and she didn't respond. She'd probably heard every word my dad just said, and now she was going to give me the silent treatment until we were out of her house. But finally, she broke. "It's crochet. And I've been doing it since I could hold yarn."

"It's okay that you hate me." Her expression lit up. Not from offense, but from surprise. As if it were a shocking thing that I knew she hated me. She didn't deny it, and I was glad for that. If we had anything, it was honesty, my grandmother and I. "I don't particularly care much for you, either."

Her fingers moved over the yarn like second nature, as easy as breathing. "I just want the best for my son and his child."

"Maybe. But you hate him for leaving Spencer." No more pretenses. Just honesty. That was all that was left, and maybe all that there should have been from the beginning.

"True. I do wish he'd stayed. That boy has never learned how to stay and deal with problems. He just keeps running from them. But that doesn't mean I'm leading a parade through the town streets and singing Spencer's praises. This town has its share of faults. Take the Winged Ones, for example."

"The Winged Ones." The words left my mouth slowly, almost an afterthought. Filling my head were the etchings from Devon's journal and a sense of vague surprise that my grandmother had any notion about what was going on in her hometown. She always seemed so disconnected from it.

She wrinkled her nose, as if the subject itself had added an unpleasant scent to the room. Her fingers continued to move her crocheting hook, but her thoughts seemed more invested in the subject at hand. "A ridiculous notion, if I ever heard one. And virtually everyone here shares at least a small piece of superstition about the mumbo jumbo behind it all. Monsters with big wings, my fanny. What this town really needs is a proper police force, if you ask me."

Standing, I offered her a nod. It was the closest thing to affection that I could freely give the old bat. "You know something, Grandma? You're all right."

Snorting, she put her attention on her work, disregarding me completely. It was back to business. "Of course I am."

Of course she was. She was all right. All right in her bitterness. All right in her hatred. But mostly, all right in her honesty. And maybe that was okay.

Outside, a car whipped into the driveway. It looked like it had once been a red Chevy Nova, but the rust had taken over to the point that it could now only be described as a brown car of some sort. Once it lurched to a stop, Scot got out of the driver's side and ran to the front door of the house. I met him there with a question on my face. His chest was rising and falling in a pant, his eyes wide. "Devon and Markus got in a fight. A bad one. Come on."

So much for planning.

"Be right out."

Without hesitation, I hurried to my room and grabbed my knife, slipping it in my pocket before running outside to the car. I jumped into the passenger side and Scot peeled out of my grandma's driveway, barreling down one empty road after another on our way out of town. I resisted gripping the dash with both hands. I wanted to tell Scot to slow down, but all of our focus was on Markus now.

Once we passed over the land bridge that led out of Spencer, I said, "Where are we going?"

Scot grimaced. "The hospital."

An ache filled my stomach. "What the hell happened?"

Scot looked like he wasn't sure where or how to begin. Finally, he spoke. "Honestly, I don't know all of it. Last night, we were all supposed to hang out at the Playground, as usual, but at the last second, Devon said it would just be him and Markus—all the rest of us had to leave. I don't know what happened, but today, Devon was pissed. He kept saying Markus was ruining 'the plan,' and Markus said he didn't care—he wanted out. Then Devon took a swing at him."

I shook my head. I had a good idea what *plan* Markus wanted out of. "A swing isn't enough for a hospital stay," I said.

"No. It isn't." Scot's eyes shimmered some and he wiped at them with the back of one hand. "I've had enough of this. I don't care if it means losing all my friends. I'm out. I can't be a part of this anymore."

In a hush, I said, "What about Cam?"

Scot shook his head, his pain so obvious it bled from his every word. "You don't see him here, do you? Here when I need him. Cam's too much of a coward to ever think for himself."

When we reached the hospital, we hurried inside and were eventually directed to a room on the third floor. Apparently, Markus's mom had just stepped out to find them some dinner, and I breathed a sigh of relief. If she could leave him here, he must be doing all right.

We stepped into the room to find Markus lying on a hospital bed, the sheets crisp and white beneath his battered skin. His face and the parts of his body that weren't covered by his hospital gown were marred with bruises. A heart monitor was beeping faintly beside his bed. An IV tube ran from his arm to a clear bag hooked to a silver pole beside the monitor. I approached him with sure steps. This had to stop.

When Markus met my eyes, only one question remained on my tongue—a question I already knew the answer to. "You wanna tell me who broke your arm now?"

Markus swallowed hard. He glanced to Scot beside me before finding my eyes once more. He looked ashamed. "It was Devon." He closed his eyes and whispered, "It was always Devon."

I clenched my hand into a fist. "Let's go, Scot," I said.

"Go where? You're not actually thinking of confronting Devon? Are you crazy?"

"I might be crazy. But I'm not running away from this. I'm the kind of guy who doesn't know when to quit. And Devon just messed with one of my friends."

chapter 17

As I approached the cemetery that night, ready for anything, the shadows cast by the full moon came out to greet me. No bonfire burned. No bottles were being passed around. And Devon was there waiting, standing several feet apart from Nick, Thorne, and Cam, who were all pacing in an uneasy circle. I walked up to him, very aware of the knife in my back pocket, and said, "No booze tonight?"

"No." His eyes were on the brothers, as if my presence were inconsequential . . . when I had a feeling it was anything but. "Not tonight. Tonight we need clear heads. Tonight we have business to attend to. Business concerning you."

"Business." There was something so old-school mafia about the way he said it. Something so impersonal. I swallowed hard, ready for whatever would come. "First I have to ask you something."

"About what?"

I bit the inside of my cheek. "About the Winged Ones."

In the distance, I could hear the lapping of water against the edges of the reservoir. It was the only sound, apart from our breathing and the brief interruption of our words. Devon glanced up at the night sky before meeting my eyes. Gone were the challenges and dares. Gone was the revelry. It was business now. All business.

"It just so happens our business here tonight concerns them, too, my friend." The last word left his lips and hung in the air between us. Friend. Something I had thought that Devon had been to me. Something that was just a word to him now.

Any question that I'd been going to ask him about whether or not he'd really killed that man evaporated into the air.

"I *know*, Devon." I hissed my words in a whisper, taking a hard step toward him. "I know, okay? I know you really thought you could bring some period of bad luck in this town to an end. I know you believe that this was the only way to fix things. But it's not."

He looked up at the night sky, and as he spoke, Nick and Thorne turned to face me. As if they were waiting for his go-ahead for something. In the surprisingly cool evening air, small puffs of fog left Devon's lips with his words. "Stephen knows."

I shook my head, so angry, so betrayed, so hurt that I had let myself believe them to be anything but the ruthless bastards they were. From my back pocket, I withdrew the homeless guy's hat and tossed it at Devon, who caught it with a look of surprise. I spat my words. "You killed that man I saw you all with yesterday. You can deny it, but I know in my gut that it's true. And for what? To appease some monsters that are all in your heads?"

"You don't really think that. After all you've witnessed. You don't think the Winged Ones are all in our heads." He raised an eyebrow at me, staring me down. "Do you, Stephen?"

"I'm not like you. I'm not like any of you." I looked around at the group of boys I had, until recently, considered my friends, and shook my head. Mostly in disbelief. "You people are nuts."

"Haven't you ever heard that psycho runs in the family?" In an instant, his smile turned sadistic. Then he shrugged. "Look. My mom's bat-shit crazy. But so is yours. Might as well own it."

I opened my mouth to deny the truth, to defend my mom, to tell him where he could stick any idea he had that the two of us were alike. But Devon cut me off by holding up a hand. "I'm offering you a way out. A life of acceptance and belonging and goddamn redemption. Take it, Stephen. Join us."

Cam echoed him, and I knew that he was speaking on behalf of the others. "Come on, man. Join us."

I tried not to consider it, not even for a moment. But it was another challenge. "Give me one good reason."

"Above and beyond everything I just said? Okay. Fine. Here's your reason." Devon cocked his head sharply to one side and then the other, cracking his neck. Then he took a step closer to me, until his face was mere inches from my own. I'd never seen his eyes so fierce before, or heard his voice so authoritative. Whatever he was about to say, he meant it with all his being. All of his soul. "Join us and you'll have a life you've only dreamed of. Join us and you'll have the Winged Ones on your side. You'll have friends. You'll have family. Join us and you'll never be alone again, and everyone here will pledge to kill for you, die for you. Join us because *I motherfucking said so!*"

He could see the no in my eyes before it even formed on my lips. I would never join them. I would never take part in whatever sick club this was or whatever terrible deeds they performed. I knew right from wrong, and I'd die before I'd lose myself in some cult.

Devon was fuming. He breathed out through his nose and clenched his jaw before speaking in a whisper so furious, so desperate that I was momentarily thrown for a loop. "Most important—at least in this moment—join us, and you'll survive the night."

Fear and anger overwhelmed me then, and I spit out, "I bet your father would be really proud of what you're doing here."

He drew back his fist, but I was ready for it. I swung a right hook as hard as I could, connecting with the left side of his face. At the same moment, Nick and Cam grabbed me, pulling me back, weakening my attack. Something hard and heavy nailed my ribs, and it took me a moment to realize that it was Nick's fist. I bent over, nausea and pain filling me until I thought I might puke. Devon rubbed the side of his face as he approached me. I strained against my captors to no avail. Then Devon balled his fist and hit me in the eye. Twice. My face lit up with fiery pain, my entire skull throbbed. The boys surrounded me, kicking and punching until I couldn't tell if it was Cam's fist or Nick's foot that was causing me pain. I didn't know where Devon had gone, just that I was having trouble breathing and it was difficult to see out of my left eye. My right cheek felt wet. The boys stopped suddenly, stepping back. "Get up, Stephen."

I looked up, only just then processing that I was on all fours in the grass. It was Nick who'd spoken. The quiet boy had at last found his voice.

"Get up." Thorne this time.

Stretching out a hand, I gripped the nearest tombstone and pulled myself slowly up to standing. As I rested against the stone, I looked slowly around for a path of escape. There was none. There was no getting away from this. From them. I was going to have to fight my way out. I straightened and looked at each of my so-called friends. Then I took a breath and said, "I'm up. What are you going to do about it?"

Behind me, I heard the snap of a twig. As I turned my head toward the sound, I caught sight of Devon. His eyes shone with a triumphant gleam. The bat in his hands moved fast toward my head. It hit and the world swirled before me. Words entered my mind, but I couldn't remember where I'd heard or seen them before: *problem solved.* As I fell to the ground, I thought I was looking up at the night sky. There were stars everywhere. And darkness.

When I woke from my haze of pain, I realized I was being bound to a tombstone. With rope. Go figure.

It took me time to fully come to, but when I did, I wrenched against my binds as hard as I could. I twisted my hands, pulling at the skin and soft tissues, not caring that I could feel the ropes digging into my wrists, burning before drawing blood. Just wanting to break free. Almost as an afterthought, I searched the skies, wondering where Devon's demons were, and when they would be coming for their sacrificial meal.

My fingers were going numb, my bound wrists worn raw by the ropes, but I twisted again, hard this time. I pulled until my skin must have split, because I felt my palms grow wet, then sticky, with what I was pretty sure was my blood. The knots were tight, but I had to get loose. Those *things* were coming for me, I just knew it.

I looked up at Devon, who was perched on top of the tallest tombstone in the graveyard. His dark eyes focused intensely on the night sky; his bleach-blond hair almost glowed in the moonlight. He had once—no, not once, many times, pounding it into our heads like we were privates in the same army—spoken of loyalty. But sitting there, with my wrists tied to the cold headstone behind me, it hit me that he hadn't been speaking of loyalty to one another or any of that band-of-brothers bullshit. He'd been speaking of our loyalty, *my* loyalty, to him. And now he was standing there on his perch, waiting for those creatures, those monsters, to come and devour me whole, not even man enough to look me in the eye.

The horrible pinpricks of numbness crawled up my fingers to my palms, then my wrists. Only my adrenaline kept them from going any farther. The air suddenly chilled. My breath came out in quick, gray puffs. And then I heard it.

Vwumph-vwumph-vwumph.

I tugged my wrists harder, struggling, hoping that the blood seeping from my broken skin might make the ropes slick enough to slip through. The rest of the gang moved past me, and none of them, not a single one of my so-called friends, dared even to glance at me as they headed for safety. Devon hopped down from his place on the stone, and after a long, hungry glance upward, he dropped his dark eyes to me. "You're in luck, Stephen. They're famished, so this should go pretty fast for you."

I bit down on my tongue, consumed with rage. A million curses ran through my mind, but I could barely speak through my fury—fury with him for all he'd done, but mostly, fury with myself for having followed his lead. I spit at him. "Go to hell!"

I pulled until I thought my shoulders might come out of their sockets, not caring that I was bleeding freely now, praying to anyone and anything that the knots would give way at last. But it was no use. The ropes refused to budge.

And then, the flapping stopped.

I looked up—up into the dark, my eyes settling on a shape in the night. And what I saw . . . oh god. My screams tore through me, my throat burning.

From the distance came Devon's laughter—cold, quiet, hollow—and his reply, muted by the sounds of my screams. "You first."

Dark shadows passed the moon overhead, and suddenly, I didn't know what to believe. The only thing that seemed sure anymore was that I was about to die.

With my right hand, I slipped the knife from my back pocket and started cutting the ropes that bound my hands. But Devon saw what I was up to before I could even get halfway through the rope. He grabbed the knife from my hand and closed it before he slid it into his front jeans pocket. "I'm afraid it's not gonna be that easy, my friend."

Friend. I couldn't believe he had the balls to use that description still.

"So what's it going to be, Devon? Are you going to throw me into the reservoir? Stab me?"

"Oh, you'll be thrown into the reservoir, if anything's left. But not alive. And I'm not stabbing you." He looked thoughtfully up at the moon, watching the skies for his beloved gods. When he looked back at me, he seemed almost dazed. "I'm not doing anything to you. It's not our way."

I spoke through clenched teeth. "Let me go."

"We can't just let you leave, Stephen. You serve a purpose. A very important one. Your sacrifice will please them. Calm them."

"Killing me won't appease those . . . *things*." I spat out the last word like an obscenity spoken in church.

Devon straightened, and pulled himself back up onto the tallest tombstone in the cemetery. Was he comfortable up there? Or did he just need for me to be forced to look up at him in this moment?

He took a second to light a clove cigarette. As he inhaled, the ember brightened and I could see that my right hook had done some damage after all, leaving a large welt on his cheek and a darkening circle under his left eye. He looked down at me and exhaled, a strange smile on his lips. Saint Devon. Keeper of his cult's sins. "So you *do* believe."

"I believe." I did. In monsters and ritual. In horror and betrayal. I believed that I was going to die. And I would have believed or said anything in that moment, just to get free. Fury filled me, right alongside fear. I looked up at Devon and softened my tone. "I believe you don't want to be responsible for murdering your friend. You've already lost one friend. Bobby, right? You don't want to lose another, Devon."

He inhaled again on his cigarette, his eyes on me the entire time, as if carefully, doubtfully, considering my words. I had no idea where the rest of the boys were or what they were doing. For now, it was just me and Devon.

Finally, he exhaled and nodded toward something in the distance, filling me with confusion. "You're right about that.

But unfortunately for you, that's not how things work in our crew. I never kill anyone, Stephen. I just clean up her mess."

I looked to where he was nodding and my heart soared to heights above the treetops before crashing painfully to the ground. Cara was approaching, dressed in a flowing black dress that trailed out behind her as she moved. Her eyes were lined in thick black. All around her, on the ground, on the surrounding tombstones, coming in for a landing, were large crows. A group of them. A murder of crows.

The look in her eyes was unlike anything that I had been subjected to before. There was no love there, no longing, no empathy. There was only Cara the taskmaster. There was only Cara the cult member. There was only Cara the betrayer.

In her right hand she held a propane torch.

From his perch, Saint Devon spoke under his breath, sounding a little scared. "I told you psycho runs in the family."

Cara held up the torch and twisted a knob on the side that started a hissing sound. Then she hit the trigger and a fierce blue flame shot from the metal tube, burning its way into the night sky. She looked at me, all love and innocence and give-a-damn gone from her expression, and said, "You're gonna burn, Stephen."

"*You're gonna burn!*" Inside the confines of my memory, Martha's voice echoed Cara's words. They'd been a warning this entire time. Somehow, Martha had known about Cara's involvement in the sacrifices. She'd been trying to warn people. To warn me.

Only I didn't listen.

Cara stepped toward me, the blue flame lighting up the madness in her eyes. She was no longer the girl that I cared deeply for, if she had ever been that girl at all. I thought of the Hanged Man card in the present position. She'd always known.

"You're gonna burn."

chapter 18

Absolute terror filled every inch of my body, every corner of my mind, every shadowed cavern of my soul. "What are you doing, Cara?"

The hissing of the torch gave an edge to her tone. One that sent my heart racing. "I'm bringing an end to the bad times that have befallen Spencer. By sacrificing you, everything here will get better."

Her words sank in heavily. I shook my head, not wanting to hear them. "You don't really believe that. You can't actually think that my death is going to fix things around here."

She shrugged with one shoulder, and as she did, the

black fabric of her dress slipped off, exposing creamy white skin. I knew that skin. I'd dreamed about it, kissed it, loved it. But that was before. The present position was another story entirely.

Her lips were pursed, her eyes cold. "It's worked before."

"Not every time." Devon spoke quietly, but I heard him loud and clear. So did Cara.

She shot him an icy glare. Devon shrank inside himself. When she spoke, her fingers tightened around the torch. "They weren't appeased by his death. And I told you to stop talking about *him*."

Devon flinched. His movement was almost imperceptible, like a single flake in a raging snowstorm, but I caught it.

"Who?" A mixture of understanding and disbelief filled me. My god. How could she? How could they? I whispered my conclusion, and their impassive faces confirmed my suspicion. "Your dad."

A black cloud passed over the moon, making the night that much darker for a moment. Neither of the twins spoke. I wondered if either of them was ashamed. I wanted them to be. I needed them to be. Shaking my head at Cara, I said, "You killed your own father because of some old story? That's . . . that's just sick."

"She had to. Everything was falling apart in Spencer. She had to do it so the bad times would end." Devon jumped down from the tombstone, coming to rest right beside Cara, as if to show me that they were on the same side, no matter what.

"And now you'll kill me for the same reason, and you'll get the same result. Nothing will change. And if it does, it'll be because of coincidence, not because you've appeased some all-powerful creatures!" The tightness in Devon's jaw as I spoke told of the guilt that ran through his veins. "You know I'm right, Devon. The resentment is coming off you like heat. You didn't want her to kill him. And you don't want her to kill me, either."

"You don't know me, Stephen."

"The hell I don't." A crow came in for a landing, just missing Devon's left shoulder. He didn't even flinch. The bird perched on top of the stone I was tied to. They were everywhere. Maybe the crows were an extension of the Winged Ones themselves. Maybe they were the harbingers. "Did she really go for help the day that Bobby died? Or did she just leave you there, trying to save your friend?"

The shadow passed overhead . . . I was no longer sure if it had been a cloud or not, no longer certain what was real and what was fiction. Devon took a hard step toward me and drew his fist back. It shot forward and connected with my jaw, heat and pain and shock shooting through me once again. He shouted, "You don't know shit about me!"

He stepped back, his chest rising and falling rapidly. As

if to calm him, Cara placed her free hand on his right cheek and met his eyes, her affection almost motherly. "He doesn't know shit about either of us."

The pain of my damaged wrists began to surface. They felt raw and the flesh within was burning. My mouth tasted metallic. I spat blood on the grass to my left and glanced at the torch, still lit, in Cara's hand.

She tore her lingering gaze from her brother and moved closer to me, dragging her fingers lightly over Devon's skin as she pulled her hand away. I forced my mind not to dredge up the memory of her fingertips moving the same way across my skin. My jaw began to throb. "You had a choice in the beginning, and you went with Devon. But then you came crawling back to me. You've been trying to get in between us ever since that first night. Choosing Devon over me. Choosing me over Devon. Always, you tried to pit us against each other. You chose to be the next sacrifice. By your words. By your actions. The Winged Ones marked you, but you're the one guiding my hand."

It didn't make sense. I shook my head, keeping a sharp eye on that blue flame. "What about the homeless man? I found his hat in Devon's room."

"A plant to lead you here tonight, just in time for the full moon. Thanks to Markus, you were getting suspicious. But I knew you'd come if I just gave you a mystery to solve. You just can't stand not *knowing*, Stephen." She took another step closer, and Devon moved to her side to assist, if needed. And oh, he'd need to. He'd have to help—they all would—because I wasn't going down without one hell of a fight. "I am glad the Winged Ones wanted you, Stephen. You see, peace seems to linger the longest if the offering really loves the person responsible. The way William Spencer's daughter loved him . . . the way that you love me. It's just a shame Dad never loved either of us."

I wanted to tell her that I didn't love her, that I'd never loved her. She seemed to know what I was thinking.

The corner of her mouth lifted in a cruel smirk. "Don't deny it, Stephen. We both know you love me. Or at least, the idea of me. And I have a feeling that will be enough for the Winged Ones."

My chest ached. I wasn't sure if it was from the beating I'd taken or from my heart breaking at the realization that I did love Cara . . . and that she didn't love me. Not really. To her, it had all been some sort of game.

"Why kill anyone? You can't really believe in the Winged Ones, Cara. You can't actually think that this town has ancient bird guardians or whatever the hell you think they are." Nick, Thorne, and Cam were spread throughout the cemetery, blocking any chance of escape. Shadows amid the tombstones. Death waiting for me at every turn. Behind my back, I pulled and twisted my hands. The rope finally snapped free without Devon or Cara noticing.

"Can't I?" Something resembling pleasure touched her lips then, creating a shadow of the person that I had thought she'd been. It sickened me now how I'd longed to kiss those lips. Cara was vile. "There have always been people like us in Spencer, reaching as far back as the town's earliest history. We're the peacekeepers. We're the faithful."

Devon lifted his eyes to the moonlit sky. When he looked back at me, he seemed almost enraptured. "You did this to yourself, Stephen. I tried to save you, to give you a chance, to have you join us instead of burn for us, for *them*. But you chose poorly."

My heart beat solidly inside my chest. Jumping up, I grabbed the propane torch with both hands, wrenching it away from Cara, and swung it as hard as I could. Blood exploded from Cara's nose as the metal canister hit her. The blow was so hard that her head flew back at an unnatural angle. She fell on the ground and for a moment, I thought I might've killed her. Then she swore loudly in a growling scream, and I knew at least that she was still alive.

The metal of the gas canister was cold from the night air, quite in contrast to its burning tip. I adjusted my grip, feeling a little bit better about my situation now that I had a weapon. But that feeling didn't last.

I turned to face Devon and he swung the bat at me hard, knocking the torch from my hand. It tumbled to the ground, its blue flame still lit. The dry grass and pine needles all around us caught fire quickly, filling the air with a low crackle. The fire spread, snaking around the graveyard and leaving smoke and flames in its wake. Devon and Cara disappeared in the haze, but I was far from safe.

Bending at the waist, I moved behind a headstone, looked to be sure it was clear, and then advanced again. I needed to get free, but there were five of them hiding in the smoke, and only one of me. The only chance I had of escape was to keep them talking. "Martha knew, didn't she? She was trying to warn me the whole time."

Cara's laughter drifted through the smoke. She was close, but she hadn't found me yet. "It's funny, isn't it? She wandered into the cemetery the night my father became a gift to the Winged Ones. And ever since, she hasn't been the same."

A sick feeling filled my stomach. What Cara was trying to do to me, she'd actually already done to her father. And Devon had helped. The scariest thing was, I believed that *they* believed they were doing it for a reason. I just needed them to see that that reason was insane. Almost gagging on my words, I shouted through the flames, "A gift? You killed him. Burned him to death. And Martha saw. She went crazy because she witnessed her own children murder their father! You did that to her!"

"He showed me he was the next sacrifice when he accepted that job offer in Minnesota." The flames crackled all around me. The noise made it difficult to determine direction and where Cara was speaking from. She was close now, but how close? Something large moved through the smoke. I was sure it was one of Devon's gang running to safety, or at least that's what I told myself to believe. If I were completely honest with myself, it looked like the giant shadow of a wing.

Cara's voice drifted through the unknown to my ears. "He was going to leave us here, Stephen. He didn't give a damn about us. But no one leaves me, and no one leaves Spencer. This town is a part of me. It's in my blood. And I'm a part of it, too. Without me, this town would die. I give Spencer its lifeblood, Stephen. And tonight, that blood will be yours."

Keeping low to the ground, I crept to the next stone and tried uselessly to refrain from coughing. I had to escape the cemetery and go for help. My grandmother and my dad could help me. We could still beat them. I spoke, knowing that Cara would answer me and reveal her distance. But where the hell was Devon? And where were the boys? "How has no one found out about what you've been doing?"

The smoke was choking me, but I kept low and kept

moving after brief pauses to check that I wasn't being seen. Cara's voice, almost casual, reached through the shadows and flames. "Oh, they suspect. They suspect and they turn their heads. They know what we're doing is important. They know that the only way to protect our own from the wrath of the Winged Ones is to give them what they crave."

I coughed against the smoke again, wondering why it wasn't bothering the twins as much. But then, they were faithful. Maybe that had something to do with it. I shook my head, clearing away such a crazy thought. "What do they crave, exactly?"

Devon chuckled, his voice thankfully on the far side of the cemetery. "Blood."

"Death." It didn't sound like Cara was correcting her brother. She was merely expanding on his answer.

A sudden breeze cleared away the smoke ahead of me, and I saw the road leading out of the Playground at last. Crouching behind William Spencer's headstone, I got ready to run for my life. Literally. "How can you be sure that there really are Winged Ones? And that you're not just murdering people for nothing? How do you *know*?"

An arm closed around my neck, choking off my airway. As Devon dragged me out from behind the tombstone, back into the smoke and into the path of Cara, he said, "We don't know. We believe."

Vwumph-vwumph-vwumph. The sound filled my ears, and I could no longer be sure if it was the sound of giant, flapping wings, or of my blood rushing through my body, filling my eardrums with its terrified song. A dark figure appeared before my blurring vision. It was them. The Winged Ones. Come for my flesh. Come for my soul.

Devon released me and I coughed air back into my burning lungs. As my vision cleared, I saw that the figure wasn't a Winged One—it was my dad, now shoving Devon to the ground, just missing the surrounding flames. I'd never been happier to see him. He reached for me, and helped me stand. "Stephen? What's going on here? Are you okay? I found your note. Son, suicide's not the answer. Whatever's going on in your life, we can work it out. It'll be okay."

In his hand, he held a piece of paper with scratchy handwriting that tried very hard to mimic my own. I glared at Devon, who was brushing the dirt from his hands as he stood. "You did this? You were going to let my dad believe I'd offed myself?"

"We do whatever we have to." Devon's eyes lit up. I could see now just how far gone he was. "It won't matter in the end what you do here tonight. Trust me, Stephen." Trust him. Trust Devon. I'd never make that mistake again. "The Winged Ones always get what they want eventually. And they want you."

"Screw eventually." Cara held up the knife that I'd brought for defense, the knife that Devon had taken from me. "You think your daddy can save you? The Winged Ones have been wanting him for a long, long time."

She freed the blade, and the metal gleamed in the firelight. In my mind, I heard my dad's voice from years ago. *"Every boy needs a knife, Stephen."* Cara snarled in my direction, blood drawing a crooked, dark line down the side of her face from where I'd hit her with the torch. "Time to appease our gods."

My dad's voice shook with the knowledge that this was something more sinister than he had realized. "What in the hell is going on here?"

A loud, shrill *bang* shot through the graveyard as the handheld propane torch exploded, its metal succumbing at last to the intense heat of the fire raging all around us. Nick, Thorne, and Cam all jumped—they'd been standing at the edge of the cemetery, looking frightened, like they were ready to run. Instinctively, I covered my ears. My dad almost fell over. All sound was silenced, except the ringing in my ears. Time slowed. Colors faded and dimmed. All but for the silver blade in Cara's hand.

I regained my senses and dove forward, reaching for the knife, but Cara pushed at me, struggling to keep the weapon in her hand. Devon ran forward and grabbed my arm, wrenching my grip away from his sister. I had to get the knife. Get the knife and end this any way I could.

The blade appeared between blurs of motion as all three of us fought for control. I heard my dad say, "Stop it! All of you! Before someone gets h—"

Cara jerked her arm back. The metal weapon sang through the air, and when it connected, tender skin burst open wide. Blood spurted from the exposed artery, spattering one of the headstones in crimson. Screams tore through my throat, echoing into the night. It was over now. It was all over.

The pain was unbearable. My knees buckled. All around me the sounds, smells, sights of night swirled into a blur. They had won. Death had not yet come, but he was already in his chariot and well on his way.

As I crumpled to the ground, I met Cara's eyes. She looked shaken for all of a heartbeat, but then her face settled to stone. She didn't regret a thing. Devon placed a calming hand on her shoulder, and they turned to walk away. Cam looked like he might throw up, but Nick and Thorne had the same cold expressions as their leaders. One by one, the boys followed Devon and Cara out of the cemetery, out of the torched remains of our Playground.

My father lay on my lap with a desperate, panicked look on his face. His left hand clutched his wounded neck.

Blood pooled quickly all around us, darkening the ground. I gripped his shoulders and tried to lift him, but he was too heavy. "Dad, you have to get up. We have to get you to a doctor. Everything will be okay."

I started to slide out from under him, my mind racing, but he stopped me by gripping my wrist with his free hand. "I wanted more for you, Stephen. Remember that. Will you?"

"Stop talking like that. I'm going to get help."

"I wanted more for you than this damn town has to offer. Promise me you'll get out, first chance you get. Forget about revenge. Nothing ever changes here. Just get out." He coughed and his grip on me weakened. "Promise."

He was barely whispering now, and the realization that I was losing him hit me hard.

"I promise," I said.

The life left his body. Sorrow and fury and loss welled up in my eyes and spilled down my cheeks. I didn't know what I was going to do.

I only knew that the Winged Ones had been appeased by my father's sacrifice. The sounds of their beating wings had stopped.

chapter 19

The reservoir looked black, even though it was the middle of a chilly fall day. I attributed the water's color to the steel gray sky above, but maybe it was something else. Maybe the water was simply reflecting my mood. Or maybe it was a sign that more bad times were coming to Spencer.

I tried not to think about that. Instead, I stood there on the cliff where Devon and the boys had initiated me into their group at the beginning of the summer, and thought about everything that had happened since the night my dad died. Since the night Cara killed him.

Behind me, in the Playground, there was a new grave.

My father's grave. I guess he'd never leave Spencer now.

I didn't hang out in the Playground anymore. The only reason I'd come here now was the note Markus had left on my window. After everything we'd been through, I still felt a kinship with him. He was like me—just a guy trying to get by in this world. So if he wanted to talk, I wanted to listen. Call it morbid curiosity. Call it need of a friend.

After my dad died, I'd half expected my grandmother to soften. But she remained as bitter and stuck as she had been before, and if anything, she became worse. She did put up a photo of my dad as a kid by the kitchen sink, but she never could bring herself to say that she missed him.

I missed him. What's more, I respected and appreciated him. He'd finally grown a backbone and had come to find me when I'd needed him the most.

Officer Bradley led a pretty involved investigation into my dad's death, during which both Cara and Devon were detained and questioned. But before long, Nick came forward and confessed to killing my dad and setting the Playground on fire. He said that he'd snapped. He said that none of the other boys or Cara had been involved at all. It was probably the most talking that the quiet boy had ever done. The twins were released into Martha's laughable custody.

Small towns protected their secrets, it seemed.

No one believed a word I said about what had happened

in the Playground that night. And since then, not a single person in town would meet my eyes, not even Ms. Rose. Spencer had become an incredibly lonely place. Lonelier than it had been when I first arrived.

But I knew the loneliness wouldn't last forever. The second I turned eighteen, I was out of here, and unlike my dad, I was never coming back. In my bedroom, inside the drawer of my nightstand, sat an early acceptance letter from the University of Colorado in Boulder. They were impressed that I was taking classes at the community college. As I had said on the application, Spencer High was just too concerned with cliques for me. Beside the letter sat my sketches, the ones I'd made based on Devon's journal and couldn't bring myself to throw away. My future, right next to my past.

Of course, most nights, when I woke up screaming, the past didn't seem so past.

"Hey." Markus's voice, accompanied by the sound of his approaching footsteps. His sneakers crunched over gravel and fallen leaves before falling silent beside me.

A group of crows was circling the air over the peninsula on the other side of the water. I watched them for a moment before responding. "I heard you're moving back to Atlanta soon."

"Yeah. Next week." We hadn't spoken since I'd visited him in the hospital that day. The one time I'd gone to his house to see how he was doing, his mom told me he was out, hanging with the boys. Scot was back with the group, too. Maybe their involvement was all for show. Maybe it was so they'd live to make it out for good. I didn't know. I didn't care. "I heard you're moving back to Denver soon."

"Yeah." Boulder was close enough to Denver to say he was right. I wished I didn't have to wait.

"Got family there?" He was struggling to make small talk that I didn't want. The awkwardness between us was so strange.

"My mom's there." It felt weird to talk to him about her. But I was less sad when she came up in conversation now— not that she did that much anyway. Mom and I had been chatting over the phone once a week since Dad's death. She'd become a part of my life again. Her doctors said the new meds were promising, so who knew what awaited me back in Denver? She'd still have to be institutionalized, but to answer Markus's question: yes . . . I had family there.

Markus nodded and looked around, as if waiting for the right words to find him.

My tongue tasted bitter. "What do you want?"

"Cara sent me. With a message."

"I don't want to hear it." It was a lie. And we both knew it.

"She misses you."

I swallowed hard. My throat felt like it was lined with

sandpaper. I had to resist the urge to ask why she hadn't come to talk to me herself. Not that I would have shown up if she'd asked. Or maybe I would have. I was still confused over the whole thing. I missed her. I hated her. Didn't get much more confusing than that.

Markus shoved his hands in the pockets of his black wool peacoat and looked at the ground between his feet. If he was hoping I'd make him feel better, he was hoping for something that I just couldn't give. He said, "Devon and the boys, too. We all . . . we all miss you."

I ran a thumb across the scar on my left wrist. It would never heal. Some scars never did.

Hating that I missed the boys, too, even after all that they had done, I said, "Maybe you should've all thought about that before murdering my dad."

"Stephen, I didn't— I wouldn't—" Tears filled his eyes, spilling over onto his cheeks, as he looked at me. "I tried to warn you."

"Oh yeah, you were incredibly helpful, Markus. What stopped you from saying, 'This group I hang with are all psychopaths. Run for your life'?" I raised my voice and narrowed my gaze, hot anger welling up inside of me, masking my pain.

Markus's eyes widened. "I . . . I didn't really know, Stephen. I mean, I'd guessed that Devon had something to do with his dad's death, and I knew that Cara wanted us to stay away from you, but I had no idea it would ever get to that point, and I—I was scared, Stephen. I still am."

He had every right to be. Markus was a soldier in Devon's army, with Cara giving the orders. What choice had he had? Still. That didn't mean I was ready to forgive him. "Just . . . just tell them if they value their lives, they'll stay away from me."

His words came out in whispers. "They might not listen."

A breeze picked up, rustling the trees around us. Spying something on the ground by my feet, I crouched and picked it up, my eyes moving from it to the crows across the water. I stayed there, perched near the cliff the way Devon used to perch on his tombstone. "I know."

It felt like days before Markus spoke again. And when he did, his words came out hushed. "I'm sorry. For everything."

"You should be."

He sighed and turned to leave. But he only got about five steps before he paused and faced me.

"At least the bad times are over now."

I wanted to punch him. But I couldn't deny that it was true, for some people anyway. The new and improved theater was up and playing horror movies again. A new auto-parts factory had opened right outside Spencer, and for the first time in years, things were looking up.

"Yeah." I stood, then stretched out my arm and opened my fingers, dropping the object I'd picked up. The long, black feather floated down in a spiral, breaking the surface of the water just before I turned away.

acknowledgments

I have always been drawn to darker things. From a very young age, I sought out shadows in all forms of entertainment. Some people are just that way, I suppose. But it was my dad, Marlin Truax, who fed my infatuation with the strange and macabre from a very young age. From the first time we watched Rod Serling together, I knew that I had found my core. Thanks, Dad. For warping my impressionable mind in the best way possible.

This book would not be what it is without the hard work of a fellow beautifully twisted mind—my brilliant editor, Andrew Harwell. Andrew, it has been my pleasure to take your hand and lead you through the streets of Spencer. It has been my dark delight to watch as you pointed out the shadows that I had not yet seen. This book is evidence of our journey, and I look forward to many more together.

My career wouldn't be what it is without the insight, wisdom, guidance, and invaluable support of the best damn agent in the world, my friend Michael Bourret. Michael, I can't thank you enough for always having my back, seeing me through every obstacle, and cheering over every success. You are, in a word, amazing. Thank you.

Sanity is a fragile thing. I am fortunate in that I have a wonderful sister by the name of Dawn Vanniman who keeps mine (relatively) intact. Dawn, you are one of the few people whom I trust implicitly and whom I cannot be without. You are my closest confidant, my dearest friend, and I will always love you and appreciate everything about you. Especially your strength and ability to overcome.

I owe every single member of my hardworking, kick-butt team at HarperTeen a huge hug and undying gratitude. Everything that every one of you has done or will do for me, for authors and teens everywhere, is so deeply appreciated. I know I will forget someone, but my heartfelt thanks go to my peeps at school and library, marketing and publicity, Team Epic Reads, the cover gods over at the art department, and the mail room guys, too.

I have always told my children that "you will find your people." It's something that I firmly believe, even though it has taken me a long time to experience. I have found my people. They are you, members of my Minion Horde. You are my people, Minions, and I wouldn't have it any other way. Together we have faced Elysia, survived the Slayer Society, fought off Graplars, and come together against bullying. We are unstoppable. Please keep being your weird, wonderful selves. And remember—Auntie Heather loves you.

An enormous part of my thanks must go to the man himself, my personal hero, Mr. Stephen King. I know that you may never read this book, but I want you to know that you are the drive behind my love of the written word. In short, if not for you, Mr. King, I would not be following my dreams. So thank you. With much love, from Constant Reader.

But most of my gratitude belongs, of course, to the Brewer Clan. Paul, Jacob, and Alexandria, you are my everything. No one has supported me the way that you have. No one has loved me the way that you have.

(Except for the kittehs. Because . . . well . . . you know.)

We have been up. And we have been down. But the important thing is that we have been together. I love you all. Thank you. For everything.